The Immigrant Train
and Other Stories

Books by Natalie L. M. Petesch

After the First Death, There is No Other
The Odyssey of Katinou Kalokovich
Seasons Such As These
Soul Clap Its Hand and Sing
Duncan's Colony
Wild With All Regret
Flowering Mimosa
Justina of Andalusia and Other Stories
The Immigrant Train and Other Stories

The Immigrant Train
and Other Stories

Natalie L. M. Petesch

Swallow Press/Ohio University Press

ATHENS

Swallow Press/Ohio University Press, Athens, Ohio 45701
© 1996 by Natalie L. M. Petesch
Printed in the United States of America

01 00 99 98 97   5 4 3 2

Swallow Press/Ohio University Press books are printed
on acid-free paper ∞

Library of Congress Cataloging-in-Publication Data

Petesch, Natalie L. M.
     The immigrant train and other stories / Natalie L.M. Petesch.
          p.   cm.
     Includes index.
     ISBN 0-8040-0991-0 (alk. paper). — ISBN 0-8040-0992-9 (alk.
paper)
     1. Immigrants—United States—Social life and customs—Fiction.
2. Polish Americans—Social life and customs—Fiction.   3. Poland
—Emigration and immigration—Fiction.   I. Title.
PS3566.E772I46   1996
813'.54—dc20   96-10622
                                                             CIP

For those immigrants who did not go on to the great universities of America, who did not become bankers, lawyers, businessmen, authors, artists, physicians, scientists, and Nobel Laureates, but who, like my mother, came, labored in misery, cold, and darkness, and perished unknown.

Contents

"I have suffered much here, I have gone the whole scale of hunger, sorrow and despair; yet I say it again and again, 'Holy America! Holy America!'" —Edward A. Steiner

Acknowledgments

"Czesio's Boots" appeared in *The Chariton Review* 20, no. 2 (1994) under the title "Czesio." "The Beekeeper" appeared in *Kansas Quarterly* 25 (1995) under the title "Stefan Zarenski."

I wish to express my thanks to the Immigration History Resource Center of St. Paul, Minnesota for their gracious assistance, and to Bernice Boksenbaum who typed the manuscript.

The Beekeeper

He had stoically endured the final interment, the reading of the will, the selling off of the farm, the surrender to strangers of the white clover fields for which his bee colonies had had a special affection, and he had, without a murmur of complaint, accepted his older brothers' decision that, Stefan, as the unmarried one "without responsibilities" should be the first to go to America. Then later (they all agreed), when Stefan had earned enough in the steel mills (they had heard impressive tales of the money to be earned in Chicago or Cleveland or Pittsburgh), he would send them their steamship tickets and they would follow him to America. Stefan had accepted this unanimous vote for his exile from his village without a word of demurral, and the following week he had endured being carted like a dead log on a wagon that had staggered relentlessly all night long to the German border, hardly stopping to let a man relieve himself. At the border—with increased urgency because he was still eligible for military conscription into the Russian army, and his departure from Lunawicz would be considered a crime punishable by imprisonment in Siberia or worse—he had hurled himself at once into the icy river and swum like a polar bear to the other side. All this he had borne without complaint—with a sense of triumph, even, over his destiny.

What was even more unbelievable, when months later in a Pittsburgh steel mill he pondered these dramatic changes in his life, was that after so difficult a beginning to his journey, he had—unlike most other immigrants on board ship—positively welcomed his eleven days in steerage. Though the seas had been violent and many passengers were so sick they could not control their vomit which flew anywhere and everywhere, including onto his own body, so that the ship's crew had been obliged to enter the steerage area and hose down the choking passengers like animals—in spite of this, Stefan had been silent and uncomplaining: the long sea voyage had given him time to think of what he might do in America.

And insults also had he patiently endured: indeed, yes —he had tolerated the indignities of Ellis Island, had suffered patiently the delousing of his clothes and the humiliating interrogation they had put him through, as though he had come to America to steal and plunder instead of to work here among the furnaces, shaping form out of the fires of chaos, like meteors being torn night and day from an exploding universe a million light years away.

All this he had endured, he thought, including this twelve-hour shift where he labored from the first grey of evening to the first grey of daybreak—the street lamps burning at the beginning and end of his shift in an eternal twilight.

It was incredible to him even now, that he, Stefan Zarenski, who had spent his entire boyhood helping his father plant crops on their farm and caring for animals—their chickens and geese, their one plow horse, and, above all

2

caring for his bee colonies, reaping from the wax cradles their amber harvest—should, night after night (and now in his second year), be the caretaker of hot metals that neither blossomed nor whinnied nor metamorphosed into any living thing. Shaking his head in dismay, he thought what a gargoyle he must appear at this moment: how, instead of a beekeeper's veil, he wore these ugly goggles; how, instead of the beekeeper's glove (which he had worn only to keep the too-lively creatures from climbing up his shirtsleeves and injuring themselves), he bore on his hands the barely healed burns from flying hot cinders; and how—above all— instead of being surrounded by his straw bee hives and his clover fields and his apple trees and wild sunflowers, here he was, Stefan Zarenski standing in Hell: a Hell not only of fire, as the villagers had been warned of time and again by Father Janachowski, but of a noise he would not have thought could be endured by the human ear.

These changes—not wrought slowly and imperceptibly over the past two years, but forced upon him like a crushing ox-killing blow from the very first day on the job— would have been so astonishing to his brothers and Teofila that they would not have believed him even had he written them about it. But he did not. He wrote them instead about the excellent clothes he could buy ready-made, and the marvels of the electric street car and about the jewelry shops downtown and the beautiful hats all the women wore, and the moving picture shows, and about the amazing doctors into whose well-furnished offices one might enter and receive treatment regardless of one's station in life, and about the dentists who could remove a tooth without pain, or not remove it at all but fill the black hole up with pure gold, and about houses that had hot and cold

3

running water day and night, with toilets that flushed. . . .
He wrote, too, about neighborhoods that he himself had
not really actually visited, with big private houses and front
lawns used for nothing but grass, and back yards in which
people grew flowers. . . .

In his letters, he revealed not a word of his real life: that
he lived in an area of three-family tenement dwellings occupied by nearly a hundred "families" (many of them
boarders); that to get water for his small two-room flat he
descended seventy-five wooden steps to a common faucet
shared by what seemed to him an entire village, from which
single water pump he laboriously carried back buckets of
water to his tiny kitchen; that the five hundred and sixty-
eight persons in his tenement area (called a "row," as if it
were yielding corn or cabbages or some other living crop)
relieved themselves in the overflowing privy vaults, the
stench of which no *voyt* in his village would have tolerated:
the indignant elders would have demanded that the wooden
outhouses be burned to the ground and buried in lime
years ago. . . . And he never wrote, of course, that neither flowers nor grass nor birds nor few, if any, household
pets were even seen in the tenements—*except maybe rats*, he
thought bitterly. Indeed, he sometimes admitted to himself
that what he had *not* written to his family in Lunawicz was
one of the greatest lies ever perpetrated on a credulous
people.

Worse yet, he did not send home any money—either
for his brothers' steamship tickets or for Teofila's recently
announced urgent need for a dowry. Although he earned
what in Lunawicz would have been thought good wages—a
dollar and sixty-five cents a day—he found that, after pay-

4

ing twelve dollars a month for his flat, and buying his groceries in a store nearby, and walking everywhere, including to and from work, in order to save carfare, the savings in his tin box (he did not trust banks) were disappointingly small. Nevertheless, he acknowledged, he would have had more than enough to send money for Teofila's dowry or for a steamship ticket costing forty or fifty dollars for at least one of his brothers were it not that one afternoon on his way to work he had made an important decision.

At precisely four o'clock one afternoon in April (he knew the exact time because he had glanced at a clock in a neighbor's window and recalled having felt unusually resentful of the fact that, though the street lamps were as usual already burning, it was as dark as if the sun had never risen), he had decided that he could no longer endure the fires of the mill and the loneliness of his separation from all growing things: that he must do something to relieve this misery or hang himself—as one despairing tenement neighbor had done last month.

It was at this moment that he had noticed a sign posted on the wall of the first floor tenement. It was apparently a copy of a law which had been enacted only the year before, proclaiming that it prohibited anyone from "the keeping of horses, cows, pigs, sheep, goats or poultry in tenement houses. . . ." "*Horses?*" Stefan scoffed aloud at the already peeling poster. "In two rooms no larger than three coffins laid end to end?" Nevertheless, he read the poster again carefully, reconsidering his options: *Nothing had been said about bees.* And he had decided then and there—even at the risk of breaking the law or being evicted from his rooms—that he would find a way to keep bees.

5

ONE MORNING EARLY IN MAY, when he knew the bees from the most populous and thriving hives would be swarming, he hiked far out to the countryside determined to find a swarm in some wild crab apple tree or even a swarm that may have—in devotion to its queen—flown too far from the colony of some less fortunate beekeeper. He scanned the horizon like a sailor looking for land, until at last by mid-afternoon he found what appeared to be a newly arrived swarm buzzing with lavish abandon on the branch of a red maple tree. He had no trouble at all smoking the bees down with his newly purchased long-handled Manum swarm-catcher, and the wayward bees having been gently persuaded with smoke, obediently entered his new Langstroth hive, which he had carried all the way on his back.

When he returned to his flat with the precious swarm, his whole body seemed to glow with a tremulous excitement such as he had not known since his youth, when the entire Zarenski family gathered together to celebrate the feast days: he recognized it now with a sigh of recognition as Joy.

What made him particularly happy was the ease with which he had managed to transfer the swarm into one of his new hives, the one with glass on two sides, which he now placed by the window in anticipation of the happy hours he would spend observing them. But he would need a queen for his second hive. So, still feeling faintly feverish, he took out three silver dollars and a two and a half dollar gold piece.

With the money safely pocketed, he left early the next morning to bargain with an apiarist, Ezekiel Toth, whose claim in a beekeeper's catalog Stefan had read was that he never used arsenic spray on his clover fields. From Ezekiel

Toth, after carefully examining the conditions under which the colonies were raised, Stefan purchased a queen bee and two cans of honey. As he laid his silver dollars down on the table, Stefan explained to Toth that he would have to feed this honey to his bees, for there were neither trees nor grass nor flowers nor even weeds near his tenement row that could supply his bees with nectar. Toth nodded as gravely as if Stefan had described to him the death of the planet, and gave Stefan an extra can of honey.

Stefan placed his queen in a little wire mesh "cage" with air spaces as narrow as flour-sifter, and carried the queen under his shirt, keeping her warm and safe: all the way back to his flat, he was keenly aware at every step of the fluttering mesh against his skin. His one concern in moving the queen into her new home was that she might somehow escape his fingers which seemed to him to have grown thick and stupid from his work in the mill, and vanish from his sight forever, straight out of the skylight he had built for her—a small piece of the sky meant solely for her beatitudes.

This skylight was an engineering feat of which he was more proud than if he had been one of the Wright brothers and had invented the aeroplane. (The Wrights' plane could fly, but could it—he asked with the silent laughter that flowed over from his new-found Joy—lay three thousand eggs a day like his queen?) He was delighted with the queen he had managed to find: she seemed to him the most beautiful Hymenoptera he had seen since leaving Lunawicz. Although she was only a common American mixture of the German bee, she compared most favorably with the more regal strain of Italian bees he had reared in his village.

When he had carried her into his flat, he set her down

for a moment on the ledge of his only window: he had thought (foolishly, he admitted) that she might enjoy the sounds of the dozens of children in the courtyard below, whose voices seemed sometimes a humming incantation as they labored like worker bees carrying endless buckets of water up the wooden stairs. But, unfortunately, this window also faced the line of privy vaults which Stefan shared with the nearly six hundred other tenement dwellers, and it had seemed to him that his queen had positively shuddered at the stench. So he had moved her quickly away from the window into the kitchen where at least she would be several feet away from the sights and smells below. Here he had discovered at least one advantage to being on the top floor. He had constructed an air vent around the pipe of his potbellied stove, which let a bit of air and light into the kitchen. This device struck him as so successful that a week later he widened the opening even further, creating a fair-sized opening for air and light, and it had seemed to him that his queen was content.

And he, too, was content, in spite of the fact that he spent so much money buying honey from Toth that the savings in his tin box dwindled to almost nothing. Although he did from time to time remember Teofila's need for a dowry and his brothers' steamship tickets, he could not stifle this first glow of pleasure he had felt in two miserable years, and he continued to buy whatever his bees needed, rationalizing that he would need no new overcoat this year as the winter promised to be a warm one, and moreover, he had given up his subscription to a Polish newspaper: thus his savings were no less than they would have been. . . .

Every morning upon returning from his work in the mill, he would remove the cape with which he kept the hives covered while he worked—having tucked in his bees before leaving as if they were fluttering birds—and would sit for an hour or two listening to his bees. To be sure, he now had only two hives, whereas in Lunawicz he had had over twenty, but he thought himself a happy and fortunate man. He earned good wages, he had good health, and, unlike so many he saw, he did not fall down dead drunk outside saloons on weekends. In short, Stefan announced to the bees: "Your master is a happy man."

HE WAS HAPPY, and he therefore considered that a simple man like himself could not, or perhaps ought not to, want more than his share of joy. . . . Then one unusually bright afternoon in midsummer, while he was feeding the squirrels in the park on the North Side, he ran into an old friend, Szymon Mazurkiewicz, who introduced him to Andzia. Stefan had already noticed Andzia from a distance, even while he had been luring the squirrels to his side with an offer of peanuts purchased from a vendor. The first thing he had noticed about Andzia, even before he had met her face to face, were her beautiful clothes. She wore a long vermillion-colored skirt with a matching hat circled with bands of black silk and crowned with artificial cherries. Around her small waist, no wider than one of his straw keps, circled a wide patent leather belt, its buckle shining with black jet beads. And on her two dainty feet, supporting all this elegance, she wore a pair of high button shoes, each black button gleaming through its eyelet of brass, like the dark eyes of his bees. She was, moreover, an altogether beautiful woman—fair-complexioned, with dark eyes and golden hair.

Stefan had fallen in love with her before she had spoken a word, and it was a great relief to him, when Szymon introduced her, to hear that she was Szymon's cousin, that her name was Andzia Burzinska, and that she had been in America ten years already—long before Szymon and his wife who were both still greenhorns, added Szymon laughing, and who hardly knew English as yet, whereas Andzia knew English "perfectly." Indeed, as Andzia acknowledged the introduction with a smile, she murmured "Please to meet you" in a voice that seemed to Stefan rich with the resonances of America.

Stefan made no effort to conceal his enchantment. He pursued her with dedicated passion, but also with the utmost respect. After all, she was no ordinary woman: starting out at thirteen as a handkerchief finisher in a New York loft, she had soon afterwards moved to Pittsburgh, where she had apprenticed herself to a milliner. At the time Stefan met her, she was already renting a basement room on the North Side where she employed two young immigrant girls from her hometown to sew feathers and ribbons and artificial cherries onto hats which Andzia bought from a wholesaler in New York. These hats Andzia herself sold to millinery shops. What was perhaps even more remarkable— at least to Stefan—was that Andzia shared an apartment with an American girl who had exciting ideas for establishing their own millinery shop—or even two or three: it was this American girl who had taught Andzia to speak English correctly and—it seemed to Stefan—with an accent as pure as flax.

Stefan realized, of course, that from the economic point of view he was definitely at a disadvantage—that Andzia might expect wealthier suitors than himself, but he knew also that he loved her, and he believed that counted for a great deal. And, moreover, he knew himself to be a decent fellow, a man who was willing to work hard and who did not drink up his money, and as for looks—well, the girls in Lunawicz had often told him what a handsome fellow he was. . . . So in spite of Andzia's financial successes he was not hindered by feelings of inferiority. He would work hard and save his money; soon he would move out of his flat into a real apartment to which, if God smiled on his plans, he might bring his betrothed. . . .

But it was difficult to put aside money for these plans, precisely because he could not look miserly with his money while escorting his beautiful Andzia to places he would not have dreamed of going to himself: theaters with plush velvet seats and restaurants with carpeted floors and white linen tablecloths where the waiter in a black and white uniform brought a corsage of red roses for the ladies, "compliments of the management." He himself would have preferred to go to some place like the Carnegie Institute, where he had heard there was a special exhibition on the recent typhoid epidemics in the city; but he had noticed that visits to the museum or outings of a scientific nature made Andzia restless: she had a way of adjusting the feathers in her broad-brimmed hat (she had recently come to prefer feathers to cherries, she said, because they could be dyed any color), sometimes removing her hat altogether and blowing at the feathers, which fluttered under her breath like a live bird about to take flight. Stefan would know when she did this that she was no longer listening.

He had never considered taking her back to his flat—first of all because he felt she would have believed it improper for a lady to visit a man in his rooms, but also (he confessed to himself) because with a single penetrating glance his poverty would be revealed to her; in short, he was afraid. But one late August afternoon—when the humid air had momentarily ceased to drop its dark veil of pitch and sorghum—while he and Andzia were sitting together in the park, Andzia had begun gazing up at him intently, her beautiful eyes filled with reproach: at that moment Stefan had proposed to her, and, almost to his surprise, she had accepted him.

A few days later, Stefan plucked up his courage to ask her to come to his flat. She was a woman, he had discovered, who delighted in gifts and surprises (she had received the diamond ring he had bought for her with exquisite little cries of pleasure): he now wanted to surprise her with his secret—the gift of his bees.

HE DID NOT APOLOGIZE for the smell of the privy vaults, nor for the mud that had accumulated around the water pump in the courtyard, nor for the stairs—anxiously, Stefan counted every step she was obliged to climb in her shining patent leather shoes. Half way up the stairs Andzia suddenly cried out in dismay and pulled her gloved hand away from the wooden handrail as if hot cinders had burned her palm. In the momentary confusion, the umbrella she had been carrying clattered to the steps below. Stefan rushed down to retrieve it, returning it to her without a word of apology for the splintering handrail.

Nor did he apologize for the narrow cubicle in which he had spent the past two years of his life. Instead, he took her hand as he opened the door to his flat and led her toward the window, where he had set his observation hive and his most comfortable chair.

"Now," he began grandly, pretending not to see how her astonished gaze darted around the room, taking in everything; taking in also, he suddenly realized, what he himself had not seen before—the nails in the walls on which he hung his clothes, the linoleumed floor whose surface was so worn that one could no longer tell what color the floor had been: only the faded hexagonal outlines remained, pale as empty waxcombs.

But he was determined to ignore the distraction of her astonished eyes, to concentrate instead on what he intended to say. "Now . . . ," he repeated. "You sit here in this chair by the window. This is my favorite place. This is where I sit every afternoon, thinking and thinking. This is where I watch my bees," he added, pushing the chair closer to the hive so that Andzia might have a better view. He then removed the cape from the hive and raised the window shade as high as it would go (the sound of its mindless rattle would echo in his mind forever). In his eagerness, he even gave Andzia a gentle push toward the chair, for she had remained standing motionless in the middle of the room.

At his touch, she folded her long yellow skirt around her legs to keep it from brushing the floor, and sat down.

"So now. . . . Let me tell you about my 'family'" he continued in a light-hearted tone he was far from feeling: Andzia seemed in some sort of shock and, instead of the romantic conversation he had been hoping for, he now felt that some rational explanation was in order. Yes, he must explain. . . . But what, exactly, was it he must explain?

Forced to find an answer to his own question, and with a recognizable note of desperation in his voice, he tried to explain: about the exquisite division of labor; the dedication of the female workers; the miraculous production of honey—a God-given gift, he added, but looked away from her as he saw her eyes narrow as if he had said something scandalous; and he explained about the bees' need for flowers and nectar and pollen, but how, also the flowers of the world survived thereby; it was a two-sided marriage contract, he added in a playful tone, hoping to elicit some response from her, but she said nothing; so he went on to describe the amazing propolis, with which the bees in their hive could destroy an invading enemy, imprisoning the intruder in the glossy, shellac-like substance so that the invader could do no harm, and then afterwards carrying the corpse to the door of the hive and ejecting it. . . . And the bees were able to do this, he found himself boasting, to enemies as large as a mouse. But here Stefan saw that he had made a great mistake, for at the word mouse Andzia moved for the first time. Shuddering, she rose to her feet, one hand outstretched in speechless protest, then sat down in the chair again, as if too weak to stand. With desperate speed, Stefan changed the subject and told her instead of the heroic endurance of the queen bee, who worked tirelessly to produce her young, laying as many as three or four thousand eggs a day. But again, Andzia shuddered and clutched her umbrella as if about to rise and flee, so that Stefan became deeply concerned, wondering what he might say that would sing the poetry of his bees and yet not be grotesquely metamorphosed into the indecency of pregnancy and the fierce reproductive struggle, and he rebuked himself for having overlooked Andzia's natural and ladylike sensibilities with regard to such subjects. But even as he was trying simultaneously to censor and sing the poetry of his bees, he remembered with stunning clarity, as in a vision, how the beautiful queen carried within her the entire spermatheca received from her lover who had pursued her with such desperate valor, himself perishing in the union. But he dared not speak of that—and even less might he speak of the miracle of the queen's body: that her tiny person was equipped with ovaries and a vagina just like . . . just like . . . (but he could never say such a thing to Andzia, he realized). Nor might he tell Andzia about how—mystery of mysteries—in spite of his queen's generous nature, of her willingness to sacrifice herself for the good of the hive, she was ready, willing and quite able to murder any contesting queen, including all her sisters in their cells, and that indeed she did this only a few moments after emerging as queen herself, upon *realizing*—silently he emphasized the queen's rational humanity—that she and she alone must be queen. But suddenly, with a rush of unwelcome truth, he understood that he absolutely must not speak of all this to a lady who was assumed to be unaware of her own decolleté, or that she was wearing—at this very moment—a radiant perfume that was as heady to him, Stefan, in its call to his manhood, as the perfume of the queen, who by her aura aroused the thirty-seven thousand, eight hundred "nostrils" in the body of her pursuing Elected One. And he knew that to a woman who probably never in her lifetime would have heard the word vagina or ovary or would dare to speak aloud of a hymen, that he, Stefan, could not so much as mention that his bees were members of the Hymenoptera. Nevertheless, he felt compelled to try to explain all this to her, if only in reassuring euphemisms, sometimes lapsing into an embarrassed silence while he carried on his internecine struggle between science and lies. One of his worst moments of silence overcame him while he asked himself whether he might explain to her that phenomenon which had always seemed to him so powerful and dramatic: how the female bees, after tolerating the idle males for a season, would suddenly turn on them and slaughter them, throwing them out of the hive like useless beggars. Only *not* useless: because all this apparent waste (he would have added) was necessary to produce the Grand Progenitor, and here perhaps it would have been possible to make some amusing comments—except that he was beginning to be certain now that his Andzia who could not tolerate his mention of a *mouse* would find his description of the nuptial flight as indecent as a description of the human seminal fluid which—if truth could be spoken—had given them both their lives so that they might be here talking together . . . but he could not say that, of course. To him, the nuptial flight had always seemed a medieval romance: an entire hive devoted to supporting hundreds of males from whose ranks a single Elected One would be chosen to give his life for the sake of his kinsmen and his queen. And although she—the queen—loved him, she could not save her soaring lover thus thrust into greatness: his death was necessary for the common good. . . .

All this he would have said had he dared; but, intimidated by her silence, and by her refusal now even to look at him (she seemed to be staring at a nail in the wall just beyond him), he chose instead to regale her with legendary tales: of how when the bees' master died, it was believed that his bees gathered in mourning on the coffin of their bee master. . . . Ah, *not that legend,* he reproached himself as he saw again the fatal shudder: clearly any tales of bees mourning their dead master she received as a bad omen. And so he told her about another legend or myth or whatever one might call it—and this one he felt sure would evoke a tender smile; he regretted he had not thought of it from the very beginning, perhaps setting a different tone— that any immorality on the part of the owner would stir the bees to anger. . . . And yes, there was still another sort of legend, he added with a suddenly discovered note of anger or challenge in his voice which he could no longer suppress: there was the *belief* that if a betrothed person walked all the way around a hive and the bees within became aroused and angry, it was considered clear evidence that the fiancé—or fiancée—was not suitable, and he—or she—would have to be rejected. . . .

At this final tale, Andzia did at last raise her beautiful dark eyes. Somehow he had not expected her to speak; it was as if he had felt she should have fallen silently into his arms, under the spell of his enchantment, his stories . . .

But when she spoke at last it was in a voice surprisingly harsh with resentment: "So *this* was your surprise? . . ."

He dared not say yes: for what else had he meant it to be but his prenuptial offering? So, almost trembling from his presentation of his most secret vision, he sat down on a small wooden stool near her chair. But this placed him at her feet, and, feeling strangely humiliated by the position, he stood up. He walked toward the window which had been tightly closed all morning, so that while he had been speaking, without his having noticed it, the small flat had become warmer and warmer until it was now stifling. Andzia's face was flushed, whether in heat or anger he could not tell, but instinctively he raised the window as wide as he could: at once the stench from the privy vaults assaulted them.

"There!" she exclaimed indignantly. "*There* is the real

world . . . the world in which your little 'family' lives.
. . ." And she rose to her feet, angrily facing him.

Overcome each one by a different sort of surprise, they stood facing each other, not like lovers but like combatants. He saw from her face that she had not received his long explanation as he had hoped she would, as the serenade of a wooing lover, but rather that—he could scarcely believe his eyes—his song of love, his gift, had made her momentarily speechless with rage.

Then, abruptly gripping her umbrella as if for support, Andzia found her voice again.

"And it was for this that you brought me here to this . . . to this. . . ." Her eyes darted for a moment to the window. ". . . to tell me these absurd stories? . . . And I thought perhaps at least you were going to surprise me with something for the wedding. But no. Not so much as a pair of gloves or a parasol. Do you think girls get married on beeswax and honey? It was *you* who fixed the wedding date for St. Szczepa's Day and the least you could have done is *apologize* to me for not having gone—no, not even once to have *mentioned* going!—to be measured for our wedding clothes, nor to arrange for a photographer for our wedding pictures, nor to consult with a priest about the wedding. . . . No—nothing. Not one word. Nothing *practical*—only stories and babble of bees. . . .

"Don't interrupt me!" she exclaimed angrily as Stefan made a vague gesture of apology. "I let you run on about your bees for . . . ," she glanced at the small gold watch on her wrist, "for half an hour or more. . . . Now listen to me, Stefan Zarenski—Zarenski, the *bee*keeper. . . . I thought that, although you had not a penny to spend on me, your fiancée, you were nevertheless a hardworking *se-*

rious man, not a man so infatuated with foolish stories of loverlike bees *impregnating*" (Andzia's use of the word astounded him, and, as if to show her contempt for his astonishment, she repeated it) "impregnating queens with a million loathsome eggs—all so that some stupid bee '*master*' without a practical idea in his head can eat—or maybe sell—what? *Honey*. And is that your view of life? Of what our life should be? That we're to work and die in the sweat shops and the steel mills and then burrow in a stinking hole like this, chewing on a piece of beeswax for pleasure?"

Nevertheless . . . , she went on in a voice ringing with contempt, . . . nevertheless, she repeated, if there were any possibility whatsoever of making money from an enterprise such as he had described, she could condone such use of his time—and *money*, she added with a disdainful glance at his Langstroth hive. She could then agree that a sane man might spend his time in such activities. But even that was a delusion, she added, because such notions could never become a *financially viable enterprise*. Did Stefan not understand, she asked, that Americans don't care one bit for honey—that what they liked was granulated white sugar which they pour into their coffee like whipped cream. And what's more, they can get all the sugar they need from Cuba. . . .

"Cuba?" he echoed dubiously, feeling compelled to utter some sound to show that he was still alive and fighting for his self-respect.

"Yes, Cuba, you poor greenhorn!" He saw now that she had dropped all pretense of affection for him and was positively laughing at him. "Cuba was one of the spoils of war, and, as a result, Americans can get all the cheap sugar they want. . . . So who would ever buy your honey? And as for living with your precious little 'family' of bees"—here her shoulders moved in an expressive shudder, but it was not a genuine shudder this time, he saw, merely an imitation of one—"I think you should get out of this . . . this *stinking* little hole and get yourself a *real* apartment and a respectable job. Working in the mill is for *hunkies* . . ."

At this infuriating epithet—one most hated by his people because of the contempt it showed for men like him— Stefan took a warning step toward her. He could forgive her her ignorance of bees, her taste for fine clothes and for entertainments he could little afford; he could pardon her veiled suggestion that the stories of his bees were mere self-indulgent fantasies—or worse—some metaphor of fertility expected of his bride: but he would never forgive her this insult to his people and to the brave men he saw working and dying beside him for less than two dollars a day. He felt so strongly that this insult to his people should not go unpunished that—God forgive him—he raised his hand and was about to slap her beautiful face, when he realized that she, too, had raised her arm and was aiming the tip of her umbrella directly at his throat.

"Assassin!" she cried. "Come one step further and your bees will crawl on your coffin!"

FOR WEEKS AFTER Andzia's departure he wavered between rage and depression, dragging himself to work like an automaton. He hardly noticed that Indian summer had come and gone, that the weather had abruptly changed for the worse, and that it was time to prepare his bees for winter. He knew only that he felt sick as with some loathsome disease. He found himself agreeing with Andzia that he was a fool, that beekeeping in a filthy tenement was romantic nonsense, suited to a picturesque village like Lunawicz, with its thatched roofs and miles of surrounding forest, but absurd in a sunless treeless flat surrounded by unbreathable air from which, instead of nourishing rains, only dirt fell, as if from the graveyards of heaven. And then, as if his own secret disease had infected them, his bees began to die: dysentery raged through his hives and nothing he could do could save them. When, one quiet Saturday afternoon, his favorite queen died, he knew it was the end of his beekeeping: he felt he would never again have the energy or the will to make another long hike to the countryside, to gather a new swarm, to spend his hard-earned dollars for honey. . . .

He began to save his money, ruthlessly putting away half his earnings. He bought no luxuries—neither fine leather boots nor gold watches; he travelled nowhere, either East or West. He ceased to write to his family, whom he had begun to think of as a gang of idle drones ready to live off his savings. . . . Instead, after many hard months of self-denial, he purchased his first property, a multi-family dwelling not covered by the new three-family limit in all old tenement buildings, such as he himself had lived in. The purchase of the new building allowed him to pack into every small flat as many boarders as were willing to pay two dollars a week to share a room with ten other lodgers. Soon—almost to his own surprise—he owned several such dwellings, one in Braddock, one in the Hill District which he rented only to Negroes, and one—most recently—in Highland Park on which he had put down a sizable down payment for his new fiancée, an American girl—no, he corrected himself, an American-*born* girl—

named Katherine (no one ever called her Kathy or Kate) who, unlike Andzia, had no notions of entrepreneurship, but who, like his former fiancée, was dark-eyed and fair-skinned, with light golden hair. Above all, Katherine was a girl who was too clever and sensitive by far ever to refer to his people as hunkies: she merely avoided his family altogether. Although his brothers and Teofila, along with her husband and children, also came to America, Stefan and Katherine rarely saw them except at weddings and funerals. Yet everyone seemed satisfied with the arrangement: now and then Stefan would lend his brother-in-law a few hundred dollars when Teofila needed it.

When Stefan was already a portly middle-aged man, he suddenly slowed down his too-busy life and decided to take music lessons. He bought a fine flute and practiced it with serious dedication until at last, by breathing in great columns of air and maintaining a firm embouchure, he could—in the lower register—produce with amazing accuracy the murmurous swarming of a multitude of bees.

The Orphan Train

My name is Marriek Józef Wesoloski. I am not a foreigner, I am an American. I was born one month after Ma arrived at Ellis Island—four days after the assassination of McKinley (Ma could never get over it: she could not believe such things happened in America). I have an uncle—his name is Stasiek—who until about two years ago lived on Henry Street: and he is still alive. So I am not an orphan.

When I was about four years old, Pa left us. He told Ma he was going to Colorado to work in the mines and make a lot of money. But Ma never heard from him again.

After Ma died, I would go down to Battery Park every day and watch the new immigrants as they got off the boats. They would almost jump to the ground, they were so happy to have got through Ellis Island and were free now to go wherever they wanted to. I used to envy them. They all seemed to believe they would get rich in America and then go back to the Old Country, their pockets jingling. But I used to wonder if they would end up like Uncle Stasiek, mad at everybody and drunk most of the time. The women, especially, made me feel sad. So many of them were dressed just like Ma, who always wore a babushka (she never wore a hat, even in church) and heavy boots in winter, just like she was still in Vilna or Lunawicz or Kalwary. She lived in our rooms on Allen Street just like she was in her own village—buying food at the market stalls, going to church nearly every day, scrubbing the floors with yellow soap. She was a quiet person, never one to brag; but one thing she liked to say about herself was that she was born on Saint Barbara's Day, the Patroness of a Holy Death. And that's what she had: she died in her sleep on Przewody Sunday, one week after Easter.

But as I say, I am not an orphan. In fact, until a couple of years ago I lived with Uncle Stasiek, we shared the same bed, and he wasn't all that bad, we got along pretty well so long as I didn't get him riled up. That happened just once— when I brought back only fifty cents from my day's work on the docks running errands for the sailors—only that one time did he ever beat me real hard (it's true he used to hit me now and then, but nothing serious). The worst part of it was, he never apologized, but stayed mad at me as if I'd insulted him or something.

Then I got mad too—I felt I had a right to be insulted, same as him—so about that time I started staying away from his Henry Street place; it was nothing but an old top-floor room anyway—cold water and plenty of rats running around the hallway, especially at night when I'd be coming in. So I started staying out nights with other boys, and Antiosek Kalinowski became my pal. He's a couple of years older than me. He taught me the ropes. He showed me how to fill a big cardboard carton with newspapers so as to make a sleeping "cabin" and how to wrap up tight as a papoose so as to keep warm on a steam grate. But the very best times of my life were those nights when me and Antiosek slept on the docks: you could hear the water slapping against the piers all night long, like someone calling you. The hard times were in late January or February when we couldn't find a steam grate (there were lots of boys looking for those warm spots). On those nights, we'd sneak into the privies after dark. But we didn't like the privies because you never knew but what somebody would come in, and then you'd have to run like hellfire. We lived this way for a couple of years.

Antiosek was what they call a "dock thief." That is, he knew how to collect "scrap" pieces of iron or copper. As soon as he got hold of them, he'd take them to a junkyard guy who was always ready to buy them. The pieces weren't always "scrap"; sometimes Antiosek just took them. Antiosek said, "We have to live, don't we?" And we did too. Besides the scrap iron trade, Antiosek was a regular acrobat with fruit stalls. He knew just how to fall over a pile of oranges, making out like someone had pushed him, and then quick as a flash I'd be under the table picking fruit like we were in California.

All that time I had this dumb idea that maybe Uncle Stasiek would sober up and feel sorry he'd been so mad at me about nothing at all and he would come and look for me. Most people in the neighborhood knew where us boys hung out. Oftentimes mothers and fathers would go looking for their boys at the Boys' Lodging House. This is a place where, if you have a few cents and you say you got no home to go to—they're not supposed to take runaways —then you can get a bed for the night. Me and Antiosek didn't stay there very often; some of the other street boys had told us that what they really wanted to do was convert us (though to what, I wasn't sure). Anyway, Uncle Stasiek, if he had wanted to find me, would have had a pretty good idea where my "beat" was. It was mostly the East River docks, and sometimes in the Italian quarter where me and Antiosek once or twice tried to pass ourselves off as Italian so as to get odd jobs sweeping sidewalks or washing windows—that way we'd get to watch the organ grinder with the monkey who came there regular. Antiosek can play the harmonica lively as a fife and drum, so a couple of times, we tried to earn some money from the crowd—Antiosek playing his harmonica and me doing handsprings—but they always preferred to watch the monkey, and I can't say as I blame them. If Antiosek and I had had a monkey, we could have made a lot of money.

But anyway, Uncle Stasiek never did come looking for me. Maybe he felt that the money I earned him didn't make up for the trouble I was to him. Or maybe the problem was we had only this one bed, and on Saturday nights if he was sober he liked to pick up a woman and bring her back to Henry Street. And, of course, there I would be, watching her close, and wondering if she was going to be my aunt. But one night while me and Antiosek were sleeping out on the wharf, I heard that Uncle Stasiek hadn't ever got married at all but had been living by himself in the room on Henry Street when one night his mattress caught on fire, and Uncle Stasiek was taken to the Charity Hospital with burns all over him. Everybody in his tenement building was driven out by the fire and smoke right in the middle of the night.

While Uncle Stasiek was in the hospital, he must have told them something about me, because it was soon after that a man from the Children's Aid Society came by. This is how it was: the first time the man came, me and Antiosek were out on the docks building a fire in a big can to keep warm (it was a real cold night toward the end of February) and cooking up a stew for ourselves, when this Mr. Prentiss comes up and offers us a bed and supper for the night. I was very leery of him, but Antiosek said, "Well, why not?" Right from the beginning I guess Antiosek was more interested than me, maybe because he'd already been on the street about five years and had had a couple of run-ins with the police who warned him that if they caught him with those "scraps" again, he'd go to the Reformatory (nobody wants to go *there*).

And then, too, the very first night we stayed at the Boys' Lodging House they started promising Antiosek lots of stuff. They promised him more than me, probably because he's big and strong for his age, where I'm pint-sized, and I guess if I hadn't had Antiosek to fight off the big street toughs I'd have been in real trouble. Still, though Antiosek was my best friend, I have to admit there were times when he wasn't as sharp as me. For instance, there was that Sunday night when Mr. Prentiss brought in speakers from out West to talk to us boys and they started telling us that we could start a new life if we wanted to, we didn't have to live like animals in the street, we could work for some good-hearted, God-fearing farmer out West, we could live with him and his children just like our own family: we wouldn't be *orphans* anymore.

It was that word that tipped me off to what they were going to do. I could see that the speakers' pitch had made a big impression on Antiosek. And almost right away after the speakers left, Antiosek and me started having arguments about it. So I was real upset, though not too surprised when about a week later Antiosek announced that

27

Mr. Prentiss had told him there was going to be a special train "all our own" going West, that Mr. Prentiss was going to take a whole lot of the Lodging House boys to Michigan right off: there were farmers there who needed help with the harvest, and that all the boys working for them would live with the farmers and have plenty of grub and go to school and be like one of the family.

Antiosek seemed not to see that this was the same pitch the speakers had made. But I loved Antiosek like a brother, and when he told me that, I knew I couldn't let him go alone—that I'd have to go along with him. Which I did. And I didn't feel too bad about it when I saw how Mr. Prentiss brought in some new duds for all us boys, including even cowboy hats. And on the train we had a pretty good time—there was plenty of grub and we ate like we were going to be hung in the morning. And while everybody was eating, Antiosek played his harmonica and we sang Mr. Prentiss' favorite song, "There's a Rest for the Weary." Seeing how Mr. Prentiss had tears in his eyes as we sang, I started to feel maybe it was all true, that Mr. Prentiss meant to do good by all us boys and was doing God's work, like he said. I was even starting to feel something like what those greenhorns jumping off the boats at Battery Park must have felt, hopeful or happy or something like that.

But as Ma used to say, "Believe only God, not promises."

It was about dusk when we finally stopped at this small town in northern Michigan, I forget the name. There were about fifty people waiting for us, like we were famous or something. Men and women both. It seemed like most of these farmers, they'd had their application with Mr. Prentiss way ahead of time; they knew we were coming and had pretty well made up their minds that they were going to take home a boy to work on their farm. But others were not so sure we'd measure up to what Mr. Prentiss had promised them—like for instance Mr. Clarke who said he'd take me home with him overnight to see how he liked me. There were five or six farmers besides Mr. Clarke who did that—they took one of us boys home and fed him and asked him a lot of questions and decided overnight whether to keep him or not. Antiosek, I learned later, was practically fought over. It seemed like everybody wanted a thirteen-year-old boy almost as big as a man who could play the harmonica.

And so the first thing that happened was, they separated me from Antiosek, just like he wasn't almost my brother but just another boy from the Boys' Lodging House. I was so miserable to find myself at Mr. Clarke's house without Antiosek that I cried all night. So the next morning Mr. Clarke told me he was sorry, but he just couldn't keep a boy who didn't want to stay with him, that maybe Mr. Prentiss should take me back to the city and keep me in the Lodging House a couple of years before trying me out on farmers. Farming, he said, was hard work—a man's work—and maybe I wasn't old enough yet to appreciate the chance that I was being given: to be saved from a pauper's life and (probably) from a life of crime—he looked me right in the eye as he said that—and given a chance to live in a clean house with decent people making an honest living. Farming was a *man's* work and not for crybabies.

But what he said only made me cry all the harder and I began to beg Mr. Clarke to please send me over to the family that had taken my pal, Antiosek, and then maybe Mr. Prentiss would send us *both* back to the Lodging House together. When I said that, it made Mr. Clarke real mad at me. He got red in the face and told me in this angry voice that I was an ungrateful puppy and that maybe Mr. Prentiss should put me in an asylum if not a Reformatory. He said your "pal" as you call him, Antiosek Kalinowski, had agreed to stay on with his employer indefinitely, that the farmer who had taken him was going to put him to work caring for his horses and give Antiosek one of his own to care for—and what was more, the farmer had promised that if Antiosek stayed on till he was twenty-one, he would give him some farmland of his own.

As Mr. Clarke told me all that, my heart about stopped; I knew I had lost my pal: who could resist having a horse of his own? So I screwed up my face real tight so as to keep from crying and even made out like I was friendly toward Mr. Clarke, so I might at least stay in the same town with Antiosek.

But Mr. Clarke had had enough of me. He gave Mr. Prentiss such a bad report on me that at first Mr. Prentiss did not know what to do—whether to send me back to the Boys' Lodging House or to take me along with the dozen or so leftover boys who had been refused by all the farmers for one reason or another (most, I noticed, were pint-sized boys like me or else those boys known on the street to be "dummies" who couldn't even sell newspapers back in the city). Because of Mr. Clarke's report, Mr. Prentiss said, there was nothing he could think of to do but put me back on the train and ship me farther West: maybe somebody else would take me. He said I should try to be nice to people and not be so "hostile": did I want to go back to living on the street? I had half a mind to say yes, I did want to go back, but anyway I had to face the fact that Antiosek would not be with me anymore, so I managed to shake my head no, and I was put back on the train. But as we headed further West, while the other boys were singing and joshing each other, I just sat looking out the window and didn't talk to a one of them: all I could think of was that now I was all alone. I had lost Antiosek who was like a brother to me. Everywhere the train stopped the other boys would pile out and run into the fields to fill their pockets with fruit. But me, I wouldn't get off the train even when they came to an apple orchard and all the boys raced each other to be the first ones out to gather up the windfall. I just sat watching them, not crying anymore, but deep down blue. As the train speeded up, everything moved past my window like a river—trees, farms, lakes, buildings, towns, churches. Sometimes people would stop to wave at our train like they knew us, but I didn't wave back. I didn't have any friendly feeling for them at all. What I was thinking was that none of their friendliness was real—it was all meant to cover up something else, I didn't know what. As the train moved forward, the friendly people who had been waving at us changed into other people—some smiling, others sad and lonesome-looking—and the countryside changed too. And the idea hit me like hot lead in my stomach that *everything* could change, so what was the use? Like Antiosek, for instance. He was my best friend, we ate and slept together like brothers; we *stole* for one another, to call it by its real name (Mr. Prentiss called it "pilfering"). And what happened? The minute they give him some new clothes and a horse he hardly looks at me, and when they cart me off to Mr. Clarke's farm *he doesn't say a word.* And when Mr. Prentiss puts me back on the train, Antiosek is so busy holding onto his horse's reins, he just waves at me. It just made me sick to think that a horse could make him forget all we'd been through together. And then there was Uncle Stasiek. When Ma died, Uncle Stasiek told Father Pomianowski that, after all, Kostusia was his sister, and he'd take care of me long as I was a good boy and behaved myself. And just when had I stopped being a good boy and behaving myself? It seemed to me now, as I sat looking out the window, that *I* hadn't changed —only Uncle Stasiek changed. First he wanted me, then he didn't—that was all.

And then, before Uncle Stasiek, there had been Pa. He too had changed. While he and Ma were in Lunawicz, he had wanted her for his wife and they had got married. Then he left for Colorado and in a short time everything changed. *He* changed. It struck me now that maybe by now he had another wife, prettier probably than Ma was, and maybe he had other sons and daughters too, who he liked better than me. In all those days and nights of being on the street, nothing had made me feel so bad in one fell swoop as Antiosek's waving me off that way; it just made me feel that the rest of my life was going to be like this train: stopping here and there, being sized up, being refused for being too small, too dumb, too sad, too ungrateful, too disagreeable, and now, a new one—too "hostile." (But at least that "hostile" was God's own truth: I felt so mad at everybody that if Mr. Prentiss had come by me with his sermons and humbug I think I would have bit him.)

But he didn't. He more or less ignored me, though he looked more and more troubled when between Wisconsin and Minnesota at every stop the farmers looked me over and then took some "nicer" boy who had learned during the long trip to say *Yes sir* and *Thank you*. But as we finally got near Aurora, Minnesota, there was no more choosing: I guess that far North they had to take whatever they could get, and Mr. Prentiss said he had managed to arrange for a certain Mr. Erik Stephenson to take me.

While we were going through the Mesabi Range, I began to feel real strange, like I had got lost on another planet, Mars or somewhere. The ground was all a reddish color as though it was still burning down there under the mud. The towns were so small it seemed they might get completely covered up by snow and disappear in the first snowstorm. And when we got to Aurora at last and I stood on the wooden boardwalk right there in the center of town—a spot from where you can see the beginning and end of it all in a moment with your naked eye—I felt like I'd come to the end of the world. Suddenly I thought of Ma: how she had lived in her little village of Lunawicz and everyone had known her there; how she had gone to church most every day and everybody had known her *there*; and how, after she died, all the women in our building who had got to know her came to the funeral and cried as if they had known her all their lives. It was a strange thing, but under that wide open sky I felt scared for the first time in my life: it was like it was the first time I really understood that I could never go back to our place on Allen Street, that Ma was dead forever. What people told me later was that I was having some kind of reaction to all that empty space after having lived in crowded rooms and packing boxes for so long. But I still think I was really missing Ma for the first time: I mean—before going to work for Mr. Stephenson, I thought I had a family; I still had Uncle Stasiek and I still had my father somewhere out West. But now I understood that the only thing that stood between me and *the empty space* was my being able to work for Mr. Stephenson.

And work I did. Mr. Stephenson seemed to have a hand in everything. Not only was he a foreman in the iron ore open pit mine, but he had bought a lot of farming land in the area and he brought up workers from Mexico to work in the fields. Mr. Stephenson put me in the fields right alongside them. I didn't know a word of Spanish and they didn't know much English, so mostly we just gestured to one another if it was time to eat or to start a new row. When we did have a chance to talk to each other—we worked from sunup to sundown—we mainly used pidgin English.

I worked for about a year among vegetables that I didn't even recognize—rutabagas and bush beans and turnips and beets and of course potatoes and onions, but the onions were small fancy ones. There was a girl named Lucía who was younger than me—she was maybe nine or ten. Her mother worked for Mr. Stephenson doing the laundry and cooking for the miners at the boarding house, and Lucía worked in the field with me. We were getting to be real good friends and I was learning some Spanish words when one afternoon, while we were pulling beets, we started laughing and talking and Lucía painted her face red with beet juice and then she rubbed some beet juice on me too. Mr. Stephenson happened to come by just as we were like having a contest to see who could put the most beet juice on the other one's face. The next day Mr. Stephenson told me my new job would be to carry water for the miners in the iron pits.

The next morning, I started pushing a wheelbarrow to

the iron pits (it was about a mile away), and all during harvest that year, instead of working in the fields, I hauled water to the pits. At the edge of the pits, I went down a long ladder carrying my bucket and dipper to where the men were working. One time it was 120 degrees down there and I fainted from the heat and was sick for a week (two miners also took sick that day). When winter came and I couldn't push my wheelbarrow through the snow, I got me a sled and hauled the water on it to the men. I sort of liked that, though I really wished I'd had a dog to pull the sled, like some people did.

When times were slack and the men laid off, I'd work in the kitchen or laundry with Lucía's mother. Although everybody called her María, her real name was Agueda (which means Agatha, she told me). She told me there was some kind of war going on in Mexico, that they had assassinated President Madero, and then her husband had been killed during a fight in Oaxaca. So she and Lucía had mostly walked up North except when they could hitch a ride on a train (she said she and Lucía would sit right on top of the train) all the way to the border. Then in Texas, some recruiters from a big company in Minnesota asked her if she'd like to work in a lumber or mining camp. There were supposed to be a lot of Mexicans like her up here in Minnesota, María said. "But in Aurora—no. Maybe in St. Paul—but here is nobody."

What María said sort of hung over my head all night long, like it was a crack in the ceiling that could fall on me: *here is nobody*. If there's someone like your Uncle Stasiek or your Pa that you ought to be with, and you're not with him, there *here is nobody*. Here in Aurora, I thought life was not so bad. I didn't have to work the docks, picking up dimes from sailors. I didn't have to knock over fruit stands to get something to eat. I didn't have to jump past the rat holes in the hallway on Henry Street. And I didn't have to sleep in a privy. All I had to do was accept that I was an orphan—which I wasn't: I still had a father somewhere in Colorado, and I had Uncle Stasiek.

I thought about it all night, and when I got up the next morning, although it was still dark (the men worked a ten-hour day, starting at seven, so I had to be on my way with the water by six), I knocked on the door of Mr. Stephenson's house and asked could I talk to him. Mr. Stephenson's Finnish housekeeper took one look at me like she knew me—though I don't know how that could have been, as it was the first time I had ever set foot on Mr. Stephenson's porch—and asked me to come in and wait until Mr. Stephenson came downstairs. While I waited, I looked around. I had never seen a house with so many windows—the windows were just letting in the first light of daybreak, and the wooden floors were polished and shining like there were lights on them.

When Mr. Stephenson came downstairs, he seemed upset to see me there. So I told him at once why I had come—that I wanted to leave Aurora, that I was going to Colorado to look for my father.

"Your *father!*" he said, looking real surprised. Then after a long silence he asked, frowning: "Was Mr. Prentiss aware when he brought you out here that your father was still alive?"

I shook my head, careful not to say too much. I knew it had cost the Children's Aid Society a lot of money to pay my way out West.

"And just where is your father? . . ." he asked slowly, like he didn't believe me.

But I was prepared for this one: I had spent most of the night thinking about it.

"In Ludlow. He works in a mine there." (I'd looked up Colorado on a map once and had seen this name that was the same as a street near where Ma and me lived.)

"*Ludlow?*" he repeated, frowning. But I could see that my being able to tell him a real place had made an impression on him, and he was starting to believe me. "And what name does your father go by?" he asked, like my father might have some kind of alias, like a robber or something. This made me mad, so I answered quick and challenging-like: "Same as mine—Marriek Józef Wesoloski," and I waited to see what he would say about *that*. But he just started pacing back and forth a bit, his hands in his pockets; then he turned toward me suddenly and said, "You can't go to Colorado by yourself. In the first place, I'm responsible for your physical welfare. And in the second place, it costs money to travel, and I would be very much surprised if you had the financial means to make such a trip." He raised his voice in a kind of question as he said that, and when I didn't say a word, he went on with what he had in mind. "But I'll tell you what I'll do. You're a good worker and I'm willing to help you. I'll write a letter to the Bureau of Mines, and to a couple of superintendents I know in Colorado. There can't be that many Marriek Józef Wesoloskis in Colorado," he added with a kind of smile.

Mr. Stephenson's willingness to do this for me kind of took the wind out of me. Besides, what he said about "financial means" was all too true: I'd been in Aurora over eighteen months and didn't have enough money yet for the winter coat I'd been looking at in the window of Mr. Chen's Dry Goods Store. Now I felt real confused: I didn't know whether to stay mad at him for his remarks about my father's name or to thank him for offering to help me. I'd worked myself up to such a pitch during the night that I was ready to start out for Colorado that very moment with hardly a nickel in my pocket. At the same time, deep down inside of me I felt ashamed that Mr. Stephenson had been able to "get" to me so quick: I was sure no other street boy —certainly not Antiosek—would have let himself get tied up like this. And suddenly, out of pure anger and shame at the awkward situation I was in, I started crying. Luckily at that moment, the housekeeper came in and Mr. Stephenson must have given her some kind of signal because she took me in the kitchen and gave me some warm buttered toast and a glass of milk. I'd had my mind so fixed on setting off for Colorado I hadn't realized I'd had no breakfast.

The upshot of my talking to Mr. Stephenson was that he did about all he knew to locate my father. He had notices posted at the different mines. He sent a letter to the U.S. Bureau of Mines about me, and one to the Colorado Fuel and Iron Company in Ludlow, and one to the Western Federation of Miners (though he disapproved, he said, of the organization). He told me to come by his place every two weeks to see had he heard anything.

When the two weeks would be up and the day would come to see had he heard anything, I'd be so nervous and excited I could hardly work. When I came into his office, I would try to not even look at him as he handed me a letter from some official person which mostly said that "there had been no such person listed among our employees." Sometimes they said they were sorry, they didn't keep records on all their employees; sometimes they complained that there were too many strikes lately to know just who was being hired for replacements: that maybe Marriek Józef

Wesoloski was a replacement, and, if so, he might be working under an assumed name. One company—the Colorado Fuel and Iron Company, it was—wrote back that they thought they'd heard of a Marriek Józef Wesoloski: wasn't he possibly one of the ringleaders in the Ludlow strike? There seemed to me so many different "voices" behind the letters that I guess I didn't really understand what they all meant, only that they none of them knew the whereabouts of a man by my father's name. By the following summer, there were no more letters. I never heard from Pa. Maybe, Mr. Stephenson says, he is dead or maybe he just didn't want ever to be found. But whether he's alive or dead, Mr. Stephenson says, I'm not being realistic—that it can make no difference now, that I'm an orphan either way.

The Immigrant Train

S tasio had been on his way to Minnesota. But once on the immigrant train, there had been some confusion—either accidental or deliberate—and the train had now been standing in the station in what seemed to Stasio an interminable and surely unnecessary delay while he and the thirty or forty other immigrants in the coach sat sweating and anxious, wondering whether the ticket agents on that infernal Island had deceived them. Angrily, Stasio stood up, trying to see out the grime-spattered window. From time to time, the train would spit steam, belch and lunge forward—a powerfull bull eager to be on its way, but reined in by something or someone. Stasio felt betrayed. Proceeding at this snail's pace, the journey would take many more days than he had money for. He had been promised a trip straight to Chicago, where, after a brief stopover, the immigrant train would go on to Minnesota: and now this.

Using all the strength in his muscular arms (which was considerable for a boy his age), Stasio managed to force one of the windows open at the top and now stood leaning against the sill, his head out the window. What immediately captured his attention, here as it had in New York, were the excited vendors running back and forth the entire length of their three-coach immigrant train, tempting the passengers with their dainties—candies, sweets or tobacco —and luring Stasio especially (his head reeled at the tart garlicky smell) with those sandwiches made of small white rolls, in the heart of which the vendor had squirreled away a small sausage covered with raw onions and a velvety mustard bright as dandelions. Stasio forced his gaze away: he dared not. If he were to succumb again to the yearnings of his belly, his few dollars would vanish like rain into the sea; his trip West would be one long hunger siege. Moreover, there had been recent rumors that, due to muddy flatbeds or flooded tracks and the shadowy but deeply feared mountains said to tower somewhere west of the Mississippi, the journey could take as long as three weeks. If the rumors turned out to be true, Stasio thought grimly, he would be forced to beg food of the other passengers, most of whom carried a bag or basket from which now and then someone would discreetly pull out a piece of bread or apple or a bite of cheese.

The immigrants with whom he had shared the coach out of New York sat quietly for the most part, the very mold of their bodies expressing a weary resignation learned long before their arrival at Ellis Island. Stasio, from having overheard, or rather from having shamelessly eavesdropped on their carefully edited remarks about their new country, had recognized that most of the passengers were either Poles like himself or Russians and Slovaks. Although one or two did seem to be "gentlemen" from big cities—perhaps Warsaw—the others, Stasio had no doubt, were hardworking peasants like his own family: impossible not to recognize his own kind in the long hair of the women, in the coarse cut of the clothes, in the sheepskin coats of the men, in their beards and boots, and, above all, in the lined, though youthful, faces seared by the cycle of winter blizzards and outdoor work under a blazing sun. Impossible too, thought Stasio with an envious glance over his shoulder at his coach companions, not to recognize the fresh smell of bread and onions. . . .

But in his opinion, unlike himself, they were already old: married, most of them, often with three or four children already, some of whom appeared to be only a few years younger than Stasio—but much shorter, he believed, than he had been at their age. Since earliest childhood Stasio had been considered a giant in his native village of Lunawicz, and even the medical doctors on the Island, although they had tapped and pried and exposed nearly every part of his body (including his private parts), had not once seemed to doubt the age claimed by Stasio at Bremen and which had been duly inscribed on the steamer's manifest list. What everyone there on the Island had appeared to want was a great grinning good health and a boundless optimism: Stasio had willingly supplied everyone he met with both. On board ship, his splendid health and good nature had been his greatest natural resource: sailors and immigrants alike had seemed willing to encourage an amiable young man with broad shoulders and a mischievous grin.

But he was beginning to think this long delay of the train was a trick—a ruse to make money for everybody except the immigrants—though he was not sure who profited most by it. Perhaps it was a variation on the tactic he had discovered—to his financial ruin—in Bremen, where the departure of their steamship had been postponed again and again, while of course the desperate passengers spent their few hoarded *zlotys* on a room the price of which could have bought them a new pair of boots back in Lunawicz.

But that someone profited by this delay, of that he felt certain. Stasio prided himself on his astuteness. He had crossed over a thousand kilometers, over dirt roads and dangerous rivers, over a stormy sea that had kept them sucked into their steerage vaults for four days out of the eleven-day voyage, panting for air, air, and please-God-more-air, while they were wrenched about in their own retchings like dying tuberculars. And he had survived these things by his own resilience, by his willingness to bend to a casual blow from some drunken peasant on the road, instead of fighting him; by bribing boarder guards so subtly that they themselves did not know he knew they were being bribed; and, above all, he had survived by trekking all those kilometers alone, confiding in no one; he had crossed an entire nation on foot until at last he had come to Bremen.

So, he apostrophized the other immigrants, turning his head from the window to look at them, as if to compel them to listen to him, it was not by being timid and waiting for Fate to send hosannas and roses that he had come this far. And he resolved then and there that if the train did not leave the station in fifteen minutes, he would go *some*where and confront *some*one and ask a few questions in his hard-earned English: he had spent the greater part of the voyage in the company of a garrulous gypsy who said he was heading for Canada, a young man whose only attraction had been that he had lived for a while in England, and had dozens of English expressions brimming at the top of his head like rich, foaming beer. Stasio had picked up a few handy expressions with a quickness that had surprised even himself: if he had had any lingering concerns about leaving

Lunawicz, it had been that the mysterious English language might prove more difficult than crossing the ocean.

He would have to count off the minutes, as he had no watch. It was the burning ambition of his life to buy a watch with (as the gypsy called it), his first "paycheck" in America: an elegant, graceful metal drapery of Watch-hood it would be, suspended from a chain of gold, which he would wear like a hero's war medal, just below the slit pocket of a tailored vest (which he would also soon have, he vowed): he had already made a smart exchange on shipboard, trading his two round-necked peasant shirts and a long coat for a stylish little satchel with leather straps.

As he counted off the fifteen minutes, his mind racing ahead, meanwhile, to the purchase of his first watch, the train gave a sudden backward lurch, seemed to tremble like a slaughtered beast, then shook itself *in extremis* to a shuddering and total stop. *Everything but roll on its side*, exclaimed Stasio to himself. Picking up his satchel—which he had not once let out of his sight; he had carried it with him even into the small urinous cubicle at the end of the coach—he stepped down from the train to investigate.

Although he had already learned to expect anything in America, he was nevertheless astonished by the flurry of activity aroused by this simple act. Immediately, he was called out to by several strangers offering him a paradise of hostels, of rooms at boarding houses, of interpreters in his own language. One young boarding house agent even greeted Stasio with a pious benediction in his native tongue. Taken by surprise, Stasio was about to respond, "In centuries of centuries. Amen," as any pious youth in his own village would have done, had not the alleged "countryman" (without pausing to take a breath) offered Stasio lodging at six dollars a week. Six dollars a week! Did the man think Stasio was a fool? No doubt of it—it was still another scheme for luring his dollars away from him, grumbled Stasio to himself, and shunned the imposter with what he meant to be a fierce scowl—difficult for him, for although Stasio was deeply skeptical, he could not really be angry with the man: he well understood the need for money. Besides, six dollars a week for lodging was such open theft as to be merely laughable. Why, if he had that kind of money, merely for the luxury of a place to sleep, it made his head spin to think of how he, Stasio, might in a short time accumulate enough to buy a small vegetable farm, or in a few years stake oneself to "mules and tools" and head out to northernmost Minnesota to receive free, gratis, with the compliments of the United States government, an entire one hundred and sixty acres of land. He sighed as he imagined the flowing acres of wheat: perhaps one could invest in one of those grain elevators he had seen pictures of in a railroad brochure.

But first he had to get to Minnesota. There he would surely find a job waiting for a strong young man like himself, perhaps at a lumber camp—he'd heard much about their need to cut down the thick, stubborn trees. If only they did not trip him up with some sly question about his age. He had had to keep reminding himself to look more knowledgeable (while remaining silent) concerning political events of the past decade in Poland and Russia, when he had been too young to understand any of it; and to keep in mind a ready explanation of how he had avoided service in the Russian army if he was supposed to be of military age; and, above all, he had to keep very clearly in mind all the details of his fabricated tale of an uncle in Minnesota who was supposed to have a farm. . . .

Just inside the station, clearly visible to all, was a great round clock on the wall with its red second hands turning slowly and endlessly, like some eternal warning signal. Keeping an eye on this clock, Stasio stood almost without moving for a full five minutes: what one might see in only a few moments in America! In only three hundred seconds, from where he stood, he could see at least twenty very different people as they passed him (and no Russian police to ask him for those everlasting "identification papers" demanded of every Pole in their captive country—in *his* country, not theirs). And all of these people passing him (he imagined), however unique, seemed to have this in common: each was intent on personal survival, on more than survival—on becoming rich and powerful perhaps. . . . Ah, five minutes of life in America was like springing off a diving board: seconds in the air, then deep, deep into the breathtaking river of busy people.

But he was fascinated not only by the unhesitating way in which the travellers walked to the many exits, but by the amazing mixture of their clothes: men wearing finely tailored suits and the gentlemanly bowler hats that were the earmark of the well-to-do walked side by side with others who wore barely enough to cover their nakedness.

"Sir? . . . Buy my last paper? I been here all night. . . ."

The newsboy had approached him from the rear (something Stasio had taught himself not to allow any stranger to do, if he could prevent it), and was now waving a newspaper under Stasio's nose, while repeating his words, accompanied this time with what struck Stasio as an exaggerated sniffle against the "cold" (it was a warm October morning, not a cloud in sight). Nevertheless, Stasio found himself smiling happily: it was the first time in his life

anyone had addressed him as *Sir*, and to Stasio, the sound
of it was more beautiful than the sight of the Liberty Lady
as they had headed for the Island: hers had been only the
promise; this was the fulfillment of the promise. During
the long journey, Stasio had successfully resisted the temptation of costly food and drink, the siren call of hustlers
from the seaport of Bremen to the city of New York,
hawking their wares to tired bodies and hungry stomachs.
But the pleasure of being addressed deferentially by a mere
boy, as if simply by stepping off the train, satchel in hand,
and merging into a sea of anonymous Americans, he had
indeed become a gentleman, was a temptation beyond his
strength to resist.

"*Sir*," repeated the boy, his expression as solemn and
honest as a church hymn at Easter, "I been here all night
and—" the boy lowered his voice to an intimate tone, as if
sharing his secret with Stasio and Stasio alone, of all the
people in the world, "else they dock us, y'know."

Stasio did his best to look as if he understood; but
clearly the gypsy had not taught him all he would need to
know. "'Dock us,'" he echoed.

"*You* know—the company. The chiefs. The guys that
run the paper."

Stasio felt he wanted to buy the paper. True, it would be
an act of charity for the little fellow, allowing him to go
home and to bed (wherever that might be). But Stasio was
not one to spend his money on acts of charity he could ill
afford. For him, buying the paper would be, above all, an
act of liberation. Although he could not yet read it, he
would be able to hold it in his hands as he sat on the train
—like a true American—and, moreover, he vowed inwardly that he *would* be able to read it by the time they arrived in

Minnesota. He did not want to ask the price of the paper which the boy had already deftly folded in two, holding it out to Stasio with fingers so yellowed by cigarettes that they lay across the black headlines like some yellowing tropical fruit, not quite ripe.

As discreetly as he could Stasio moved toward a small secret pocket in his pants and pulled out a nickel.

The boy's voice, still unbroken as a choir boy's, seemed suddenly to crack with chagrin: "Don't have any change. Gave my last two coppers to that little cigarette girl over there—see the one with the tray round her neck? She's my girl . . . I mean, if I *wanted* her to be, she'd be. She's a little young, though," he added, slewing his gaze as if in pious protectiveness toward the girl.

Stasio, overcome by involuntary admiration for this performance, waved aside the change with what he felt was the proper disdain of a newly made gentleman like himself, and stood for moment staring at the black letters which were as meaningless to him as the Russian-language textbooks the government had forced upon them. He had expected that the saucy little fellow with his carnival performance would walk away, content with having gulled Stasio out of at least two pennies. But instead, the boy stood watching him a moment.

"Hey mister!" the boy exclaimed in a tone of sharp surprise but also with a note of unexpected admiration, as if the newsboy now knew something about Stasio that made Stasio quite as extraordinary a fellow as himself. The boy hesitated a moment, as though in spite of his mountebank strategies he were fighting with an (unaccustomed) honest impulse. "Mister," he whispered. "Why don't you let me fix this for you?"

49

Stasio was always afterwards to remember that the boy had said this without irony or derision, but indeed with a mixture of compassion and complicity, as of one beggar spotting another in a crowded square.

As the boy rearranged the paper which Stasio had been holding upside down, Stasio blushed to the roots of his hair. His eyes blurred over with shame, while at the same time, as if by an act of witchcraft, he was suddenly able to read part of the headline that was to be imprinted on his memory forever: PRESIDENT TAFT AND PORFIRIO DIAZ WILL. . . . He was never to learn what President Taft and the leader of Mexico were planning that year, but he was never to forget the shock to his senses from the black and white page, as if the dark sky of his mind had suddenly been torn by sheet lightning. Still, in spite of this unmasking, Stasio managed to look down at the bright brown eyes of his companion and calmly recite his gypsy-taught phrase: "Thank you very much for your assistance in this matter."

And the boy did not laugh. Instead, suddenly, the whining tone and hypocritical deference were wiped away like so much vaudevillian makeup after the show, and the feigning man-child became transformed before Stasio's eyes into a real child. The boy, looking up into Stasio's blue eyes, at his broad, strong shoulders, and his air of self-confidence that was even greater than his own, seemed to drop all subterfuge, as if acknowledging that his own audacity, his saucy routine of mirth, lies, and deference, were nothing but a thing of gauze that he was happy to drop before a superior artist.

"Jeez," he exclaimed with honest awe. "Where you come from, greenie? A long ways, huh?"

Ignoring the offensive "greenie"—a word he already knew too well—Stasio answered, not without pride: "From Lunawicz. Poland. Maybe five thousand kilometers!"

"You come *alone?*" The newsboy's admiration was so genuine that Stasio's pride was greatly mollified. He tried, therefore, to explain that he was now headed for Minnesota where strong men—he blinked conspiratorially at this description of himself—were needed, hundreds of them, to chop down an endless forest of trees. He opened his arms wide in an attempt to describe the boundless horizon of trees.

The boy rolled his eyes, as if more pained than impressed by this image of an unpeopled wilderness. "And how much money will you make," he demanded to know, "doin' that hard work a million miles from nowhere and livin' in some barracks where they don't even have any girls—I'll betcha *that?*"

For a few moments, though Stasio had not understood half of what the boy was saying, Stasio was struck dumb. Clearly, the fact that there would not be any girls in the lumber camps had not entered sufficiently into his calculations. And the realization that he would be more or less isolated from the world, without wife, mother, sister or sweetheart to ease his days (as to nights, Stasio had had little experience, though he had been initiated this year by a "loose" woman of his village) now struck him with troubling force.

But the newsboy apparently thought that Stasio had not understood him. So he tried again, reducing his words to a minimum and adding a pantomime of Despair and Loneliness.

"No girls!" He rolled his eyes for emphasis. "Hard

work!" He bent his small back and grunted, then straightened up as if with an effort. "How much money? Dollars? Paycheck? How much?"

Ahhh . . . of course. The magical "paycheck." But Stasio really didn't know—only that it was sure to be astronomical compared to what his father had eked out on their small farm. He shrugged, trying to look philosophical about it, but embarrassed not to have the facts concerning such an important detail.

"Huh! You know what I make?" boasted the boy. "My *own* paycheck? Just sellin' papers for myself I make more 'n a dollar day. But what's more, I got two boys workin' for me. I pay them two bits a day—they bring me in somethin' for every paper they sell. Mostly they just hop the street cars, they don't have a corner like me. But listen, none of them is cooped up in no camp, cuttin' down big logs for cabins where you freeze your butt off for years and years maybe before you even get a nice warm place to sleep in. . . . Nah, here in Philly a guy gets to see some action, y'know what I mean? You should come with us just one night I tell you, down to the tenderloin district. Of course *you* probably think the tenderloin is a steak, right?" And he laughed merrily, his dark eyes bright with secret knowledge. "And lots of nights we don't do nuthin'. Nuthin! No work at all," he emphasized. "We just lay around the newspaper building, waiting for The Big Rush—that's the morning rush, y'know, you got to be right there to pick up your papers at three in the morning 'cause the guys in the street, they want their papers by four o'clock. Or maybe it's your factory guy just comin' off the graveyard shift—first thing they grab is *my* paper. . . ." He paused, breathless, scanning Stasio's face to see if he had been as impressed as he should have been by all these confidences.

But Stasio, though hypnotized by the running patter and occasional pantomime had not understood much beyond "No girls! Hard work!" Astonished, he felt he had not merely bought a newspaper but had tapped into a secret source of information—someone who, if Stasio had time to listen to him, could unlock for him the treasures of America. But now, looking beyond the boy's questioning gaze toward the opposite wall, Stasio was stunned to realize that ten minutes had gone by during which, held spellbound by the newsboy, he had forgotten to watch the clock.

"I go! I go!" he exclaimed wildly. Frantic with anxiety, he turned to run, the satchel banging his knee as he hurled himself toward the door, his brain tolling like a funeral bell: *You fool. You worm. You peasant. You clump of dirt and dung.* He crashed through the door to his departure platform, dreading to see what years later he judged to be his destiny.

The platform was deserted. The train had gone.

Never had he felt such despair. No, not when he was seven, and his father had beaten him nearly senseless for having forgotten to lock the cowshed and their only cow had wandered away to freeze to death overnight; not when his older brother, so strong and protective of Stasio, had disappeared into darkest Russia while serving his compulsory five years' military service; not when he himself, only recently, had lain sick and hungry as a hyena on the stones of a creek bed, hiding from the Russian police who did not want him to leave Poland but wanted him too, like his brother, to eventually disappear in the dungeons of Russia. And no—not even when, with a sigh of pain, his fragile mother had sunk to the earth before his eyes, never to rise again. . . .

He stood motionless: he did not know exactly where he

was in America; he did not know the laws of this land; he did not know but that what he had done—descended from what seemed to be some officially assigned immigrant train —was illegal, something for which they could deport him; he did not know the language. And he did not have enough money to feed himself, even for a few days.

At last he sank to a bench, staring still at the empty tracks. He sat hunched and humiliated, his body a mere hulk that was suddenly more of a burden than a blessing, for such mighty muscles would soon make their tyrannous demand to be fed. So he sat dumbly, his throat clenched with silent sobs. And he thought—perhaps for the first time in his life—of the reality of death. Yes, it was possible to die in America, of despair if not of hunger. He shut his eyes against the October light, wondering if perhaps he were fated to die right there at that moment on this bench. . . .

He open his eyes again at the touch of a hand on his shoulder. It was the newsboy—suddenly deferential again. "C'mon with me. I got a place." He picked up Stasio's satchel; he beckoned so that Stasio would understand that he was to follow. Stasio followed: he was so numb he did not even consider it odd that a dark-haired newsboy—so small that he might have been a royal dwarf—was carrying Stasio's satchel while Stasio, half-dazed, an obedient giant, followed after.

"This ain't so heavy," confided the boy, as if recognizing and explaining the strange phenomenon: "Jeez, I carry forty pounds of papers a night, y'know?"

THEY SAT ON THE FLOOR of the boy's room, eating pickles and doughnuts. His name was Gem. He said he had lived in the streets for several years after his stepfather had kicked him out, but for the last six months or so he'd had this room. He explained that he had received his nickname (his real name was William) from one of the "ladies of the night" who had once remarked that he was a "real gem to have around." He occasionally ran errands for this lady and for several others when they needed something special (here Gem made a few gestures which were meaningless to Stasio). The ladies, he added, preferred him or one of his newsies to the regular telegram messenger boys who, his lady had told him, talked too much and sometimes spilled the beans. "You'll see—I'll take you along. It's just a little something extra—like free peanuts in a saloon. Like listen: I might go get a small jarful for her—maybe about this size" —he curved his yellow-stained fingers into the shape of a slender quarter moon; "I pay, maybe a buck and a quarter for it, and she always lets me keep the change. Always. No big deal for her, y'know? Look, you stay here tonight, and tomorrow I'll show you around. Saturday's the best night anyway. I promise you you'll have the time of your life." He laughed. "Just one night in Philly and you'll forget all about those big trees and log cabins. . . ."

The following night Gem kept his promise and took Stasio with him everywhere. Saturday night was theater night in Philadelphia, and by eleven o'clock he and Gem were awaiting the release of the show crowd. Many of them, Stasio observed, flowed out of the theater in a rush of laughter which became instantly subdued as the two boys approached, the eyes of the women widening with guilt and something like fear. That night, he and Gem sold dozens of papers, and Stasio was quick to note how often Gem managed to make errors in returning the change.

Sometimes the men would stand for a moment looking down at the "mistake" in the change, then with a shrug of boredom or melancholy—Stasio wasn't sure which—they would hurry the woman into a taxi as if it were they who had just tricked Gem out of his money rather than the other way around, and they had to make a quick getaway.

After watching about an hour of this sort of thing, Stasio felt that he in Gem's place could have done even better than Gem: merely by using a time-honored sleight of hand, one might easily confuse the two-dollar bills with the fives. From there, later that night like boys at a circus, they went merrily to the red-light district, knocking at the door of the one house in particular where Gem and his newsies had contacts. Not on that night, nor on the next, nor the next was there any talk of the immigrant train. Instead, Gem concentrated on teaching Stasio all he knew, and he knew a lot. It seemed no time at all before Stasio had learned all Gem's skills and could turn a dollar as quickly as his friend, though at first he had a little trouble adjusting to the ladies. During his first few "house calls" (as Gem referred to them, as if he and Stasio were doctors), Stasio would avert his eyes from the girls' nudity, or stand mute and startled at the sight of their lovely young mouths opening into a wide gaping hole as they yawned with boredom and yearning for cocaine. But Stasio was an apt pupil. He soon learned that if he ran quickly enough to get these listless ladies their needed jolt of coke—paying six dollars for the cocaine and two dollars for the hypodermic needle—that when he handed them their change from a ten dollar bill, they would merely make a mocking little moue at him, preferring to kiss him or tease him instead. Or, if sometimes they had been lying lifelessly in bed until his return-

lying with those soft white arms which seemed never to have held anything heavier than a man's open mouth motionless above their heads—they would nevertheless rise with joy when he returned with their precious purchase, opening their arms to him in gratitude: their armpits, Stasio noted, were always shaven clean as a skull, and of a pure white, never touched by the sun. They reminded Stasio somehow of the Easter lilies behind the altar of the church in Lunawicz, where such sins of the flesh were so far removed from the imaginations of Father Pankiewicz's kneeling parishioners that the good priest did not even trouble himself to rail against harlotry, but was in the habit of speaking, rather, about not stealing and of honoring thy father and mother.

On Stasio's very first Saturday night of working alone without Gem to clue him or prompt him, he earned as much as the younger newsies made in a week. When he reported this to Gem, his friend was impressed. Looking forward to the future, he and Gem foresaw a time when they themselves would no longer have to sell newspapers—when a crew of others would do it for them.

And it turned out as they had foreseen. He and Gem became loyal partners. First they paid out fifty dollars for a better corner, and held on to it fiercely, refusing to let it go to anyone at any price, until business was so good they soon had four more newsies working for them, all recruited from Gem's nearby school (true—the boys had to stick to the letter of the law, attending school for three hours a day; but so long as they sat through this obligation, they were free to work all night for Gem). Gem paid his classmates a dollar a week, but a lot of them made much more through their own cleverness. They and their newsies were prospering: things looked so good that Stasio and Gem talked of expanding, of creating a real, lifetime partnership.

Stasio soon forgot all about Minnesota, which, anyway, he never found time to visit, so he never felt he had missed anything much; but he did get up to Michigan once, where he'd heard from some stranger that many Poles had settled in Hamtramck, maybe some of them from Lunawicz. But when he arrived, there was no one who had ever been near Lunawicz, and no one knew a soul by his family name.

He returned from Michigan somewhat disappointed. But on his way back to Philadelphia, while on the train, Stasio had a vision or a dream of his village which was to recur now and then all the rest of his life: of a field of honey-colored wheat through which soughed the fall winds of Lunawicz till the entire land seemed to frolic and dance, making a singing sound as of swarming bees. And throughout the vision he could distinctly hear the cry of birds: Stasio even thought he recognized the storks that used to roost on Father Pankiewicz's roof beside the church, and recognized, too, the honk of the pampered geese heading for the pond near the house of one of the most respected old men of the village. And in this dream he stood on a hillside from where he could see the entire lie of the land along Lunawicz: the yearning willow trees dipping their boughs into the river; the swimming places along the river where, when a day's work was over, he and the other boys would plunge their naked, sweating bodies; and above all— as his soul wafted between vision and dream—he could hear the sound of his horse, Wenzel, neighing with delight as Stasio fed him a rare bit of carrot out of his own hand. In response to the soft nibble of Wenzel's mouth on his palm, Stasio would rise from a deep sleep and cry out

Wenzel's name. But always the vision retreated as he and his horse made their way toward the barn. The barn door would open as if of itself, and Stasio would set his right foot across the threshold which would turn out to be a platform and the station would be empty, for the train had gone.

Czesio's Boots

Czesio's new boots had been stolen from him on board ship—boots which had cost him three weeks' labor in a bakery over forty wiorstas from his village, working nights and sleeping on a stove alongside the rising dough: vast pyramids built during the deep silences of a village night. His employer would not permit Czesio so much as a candle to light his way around the basement for fear of fire, and often, feeling enveloped by these phantom shapes, it had been difficult for Czesio, in spite of his exhaustion, to fall asleep. So, surrendering himself to sleepless nights, he would lie on the stove, his hands behind his head, imagining that he was already moving along that jade-colored highway leading to New York and onward to the unimaginable territories of the West.

His parents had at first objected to his taking work outside Lunawicz, complaining that he would be needed for spring planting (though Czesio had understood that they were ashamed, also, to have him work for strangers, away from their own village). Czesio, however, had argued that he could not wear his shabby old boots to a country from which other young men of Lunawicz had returned with the gold in their teeth gleaming every time they opened their mouths: at the very least, he added, he would need a new pair of boots; and so, after several arguments, his parents had consented. Czesio had had himself measured for the boots by their village cobbler even before leaving, and upon his return had paid for them with the *zlotys* he had saved every day for so many weeks. Wearing the new boots, Czesio would walk around their cottage and often (except on rainy days) would pace back and forth on the path between their cottage and the bee colony his father kept at the edge of their small farm.

The boots were perfect; Czesio polished them every night before going to bed, and it pleased him to see how they reflected the sunlight by day. From time to time, as he leaned over the bee hives to listen to the faint hum within, he thought with pride how his boots were exactly the color of the honey being laid, day after day, through God's generosity, among the waxy honeycombs. It had seemed to him a good omen.

However, it turned out to be ten long months before his brother Henryk was able to keep his promise to send Czesio a steamship ticket, and by then it had turned bitter cold. On the day of his departure, the sky in Lunawicz was overcast and the bare trees were layered with ice as he and his parents walked to the outskirts of the village. His mother stood shivering with cold and grief in the frozen path which Czesio would take to the train. She had not stopped crying since the ticket had arrived from Henryk, and she vowed to curse the steamship company and their agents with her last breath for luring first Henryk and now her younger son to that godless country. Czesio's father, however, stood erect and stoical, and reminded him to send home money when he could, for his sister Pecia would soon need money for her dowry. Then, to soften his words, and trying also to be cheerful, he had asked Czesio how he felt in his new boots.

The truth was (though Czesio would not for anything have confessed it), that while waiting all those months for the ticket, Czesio's toes, with the secrecy of the leavening dough in the bakery, had grown longer even as Czesio himself had grown an inch taller—as if the very prospect of going to America had mysteriously added a cubit to his stature. But when his father asked him about the boots, Czesio declared that they were perfect.

On board ship, however, Czesio found that the boots pinched when he tried to swing his body pendulum-wise on the rolling deck. He endured this discomfort until the third day at sea. Then, on that afternoon, when he and about three hundred other men with whom he shared the steerage bunks below came up on deck after a severe winter storm, he acknowledged to himself that the boots were no longer a source of pride but of torture. He sat down on a pile of rope and began pulling off, first his boots, then his dank socks. And it was while he was rubbing his long toes in the cold fresh air that he noticed—not for the first time—the girl in the rose-colored shawl.

The girl glanced for a moment at his bare feet—Czesio thought he had seen on her lips the faintest of smiles—then returned at once to her book, the same book she had been reading since they first set out from Bremen.

What Czesio had first noticed about the girl—besides the fact that her long hair was still uncut and she wore a fully pleated skirt which covered her ankles—was that instead of a basket or valise she carried a beautiful bag made out of plain cotton cloth, but lavishly embroidered with birds and flowers. It was from this bag that she would carefully take out her book every day and read for an hour or two. At first Czesio had thought it must be a holy book, because his mother, too, would often keep her Bible open for hours at a time, particularly during Lenten season.

As he sat rubbing his still-aching feet, he continued to observe the girl as unobtrusively as he could, noticing especially her slender white hands, so unlike his own rough hands, calloused from laboring in the fields. And he was imagining for a moment, in a kind of daydream, how it might be to have those soft white hands touch one's face, when abruptly the girl pressed the open book to her bosom and Czesio saw that it was in English.

In English! Czesio nearly moaned aloud with envy. What would he not give to know the language of that vast country! And then suddenly, besides envy, he felt a strange new emotion: he wanted, with a sort of nostalgic longing as if he already knew the sound of her voice but yearned to hear it again, to hear her speak; but probably this educated girl who could read English would not want to talk to a peasant like himself who had barely received a few years of schooling . . .

It was while Czesio had been waiting to see if the girl would speak—if not to him, then to someone else, so that he might hear whether she would speak in some foreign tongue or in Polish—that some thief had stolen his boots.

The girl had witnessed the theft. She rose to her feet calling out, "Stop!" and Czesio was so pleased to hear her voice and to recognize his native tongue that he did not even look around him to see what was happening. Within moments the thief had vanished forever, fading into anonymity among over a thousand passengers. Though Czesio reported it, the ship's crew was indifferent, pointing out that they might search all the boxes, baskets and trunks in steerage yet never find the boots: as a last resort, they told him, the fellow could simply chuck the boots overboard. But Czesio was far from inconsolable: the girl had spoken and he soon discovered, to his joy, that she came from a village not far from his own. Indeed, since his family rarely travelled, owning neither horse nor ox, it struck Czesio as something like a holy mystery that he had even once been in her village: Czesio then described to her how he and his brother Henryk and his sister Pecia, along with their parents, had walked the entire distance from Lunawicz in order to attend his aunt's funeral. Not wishing to seem to boast of any heroic effort on his family's part, Czesio added quickly that it had been summer, of course, and they had had good weather. When he saw how the hazel eyes filled with tears as he told her this, Czesio fell in love.

He and Theodora—for that was her name—spent the next ten days of what would otherwise have been a miserable crossing, with fierce winter winds, joyfully talking together. Czesio discovered speech: he had not known what an eloquent fellow he could be until he met Theodora. But his voice trembled when at last he steeled himself to ask the most vital question of all: "And . . . and . . . you have someone there? I mean, someone will be waiting for you when the ship arrives?"

She shook her head.

"But how will you . . . ?" He hesitated, feeling relieved that she had no fiancé awaiting her, but also anxious for her sake that there would be no one to greet her. He had heard rumors in his village that a woman who arrived alone at Ellis Island could be detained—in a wire cage!—that if she did not prove to the satisfaction of the immigration officers that she was a respectable lady, they could even deport her. At the mere possibility that Theodora might be deported, his heart raced anxiously; but he managed to repeat his question without frightening her with such rumors.

At this, Theodora drew a letter from her bag (Czesio was greatly relieved to see that the letter was not in English), explaining, "This is from my sister Aleksandra. She lives in the northern part of America. In Massachusetts," she added, glancing at him to see if this had any significance for him. But to Czesio the strange name meant only that she was not going West. "Ah," he protested fervently, "but I am going to Colorado!" and with these few words he understood that he had revealed both to her and himself that he wished desperately that she not go where he was not—that he would try to dissuade her from going to that strange-sounding place.

Theodora looked at him intently a moment, without saying anything; then she unfolded the thin, densely covered pages and began to read the letter to him in its entirety.

Aleksandra's joy at having come to America, and especially to Massachusetts, was absolute. Here, she wrote, girls could get good jobs at good wages; they could live in well-managed, respectable boarding houses; there were educated girls in Massachusetts who worked in clean clothes and even had a literary magazine all their own. In America, she wrote, you could be any thing you wanted, and people would not call you a *wh----*here, evidently, Aleksandra had faltered at writing such a word, and an attempt had been made to cross out the shocking letters—just because you lived away from your family. You could be a street car conductor if you wanted to—or a factory worker. Why, in seven states already women could vote! Theodora, too, her sister went on to say, could do as she had done: first she had worked in a textile mill; then she had gone to night school and taken lessons on a typewriter, and now she had a "position" in an office where she worked for a doctor. And finally, she wrote, having saved her greatest surprise for last, she was going to buy a brand new Ford automobile. This was too much for Czesio and he exclaimed: "No, no, no. I do not believe it. It is too good to be true!"

Theodora, to persuade him, and perhaps also because she was somewhat hurt that Czesio had not accepted her sister's word for it all, now placed a photograph in Czesio's hand and sat looking at him in silent triumph.

The photograph revealed a smiling, slightly older version of Theodora sitting before a machine, her hands delicately poised over the rounded keys. Looking at it very closely, Czesio could see the decorative-looking letters REMINGTON painted in white on the glossy black metal surface of the machine. But it was Theodora's sister who most astonished him—a girl who in five short years had created a new life for herself: with her long hair swept upward and arranged in a sepia-colored crown at the top of her head, with her round white collar starched to perfection and set off by a small bow, with the sleeves of her striped blouse gathered delicately at the wrists by a pair of gleaming cufflinks, she looked every inch a fashionable lady from a great city. But even more than by her ladylike apparel, Czesio was struck by the self-confident cast of the head, the frank open manner, the knowledge revealed in the hazel eyes that met his own with undaunted intimacy, telling secrets women were never meant to reveal. . . .

In spite of his awe, Czesio managed to repeat, "It is all

too good to be true, Theodora. It cannot be. Life would be a paradise if all this were true." And then, not to be out-done by a typewriting machine which turned peasant girls into ladies overnight, he had just begun to tell Theodora about the excellent wages he and his brother Henryk would be earning in the Colorado mines when the dinner bell rang thoughout the steerage deck.

"We must talk about this again, Theodora. But right now, you must eat," he declared. And he began at once to shield her, as if he had an inherent right to do so, from the rush of hungry passengers, most of whom had not eaten since before the storm.

He hoped that for Theodora's sake they would have something better to eat that day. But his heart sank as he saw again in their iron pots the same stew of yesterday and the day before. When he had first smelled the rancid meat and seen the few floating pieces of cabbage, he had felt a rush of nausea; but because he had not had the foresight to bring any food of his own, he had been forced to muster his courage and eat the stew. And Theodora, too, he now discovered had been improvident. She had carried all the way from her village a consecrated image of the Madonna of Czestochowa, an embroidered tablecloth for her sister, and the books her sister had sent her, including the gram-mar book Czesio had seen her with. But she had brought no food of her own. She admitted to Czesio that she was very hungry, that she had been quite unable to eat anything served up to them on board ship, and so had had nothing but tea and bread since leaving Bremen. Czesio exclaimed that she could not continue in this way, that she would be ill, that he would find decent food for her somehow, even if he had to ask among the other passengers. And he did so, bartering what few articles he had brought with him for a cucumber, an apple, a piece of cheese. Thus he became—as he himself declared—her Protector: he said that he would not allow Theodora to be shoved about by the crowds on deck; that he would carefully examine her steerage blanket every morning to be sure that no vermin had made their way to it from the blankets of other passengers; and above all, he assured her, he would see to it that no male passengers should speak to her disrespectfully merely because she was a girl alone. Theodora smiled gratefully at this gallantry; but from her silence, Czesio understood that she meant to continue her journey northward.

For the rest of the voyage Czesio pondered his future, and how it would be without her. He felt that she was perfectly right to join her sister; but was he also not right—indeed, obligated—to go on to Colorado where his brother had told him that he and Czesio together might earn in a day more than their father in a month? And moreover, Henryk had assured him, soon they would not be working such long hours, but would have an eight-hour day like miners elsewhere. But as the days of their sea voyage passed, during which he and Theodora spent nearly all their waking hours together, Czesio felt that he could not be separated from this girl. So at last, only a day before their arrival, he proposed to Theodora. And when he said he understood very well that she could not give up a promising future with Aleksandra to go and live with him in a rough mining town, so if she would marry him, they would go together to join her sister, Theodora bowed her head in assent, weeping with joy.

So they were married on Ellis Island, he and Theodora and at least a dozen other couples with them. On the train north, they sat together all the way, holding hands. From time to time, in a tender transport of unbelief at his good fortune, Czesio would kiss the ringed hand by which his beloved had bound herself to him forever, clasping it urgently to his bosom, as if some thief might bear it away.

As the train neared their destination, it slowed down: it seemed to pause every few hundred feet, as if meditating whether it should finally complete their long journey. Theodora, tense with excitement at the thought of seeing her sister for the first time in five years, kept looking out the window every few minutes to see if they had yet arrived. "Why should it take so long?" she murmured, and it struck Czesio that it was the first time he had heard her complain of anything.

But he was asking himself the same question. He tried to open a window but, perhaps because of the bitter February cold, they had been tightly locked. "Be patient, Theodora," he said reassuringly. "We are almost there."

At last the train inched its way into the station. Czesio picked up their new valise and they threaded their way down the aisle to the door of the train. Theodora began weeping silently, overcome with joy that they had reached the end of their long voyage.

But she did not see her sister. She looked around the station for a moment with a worried look, murmuring in defense of Aleksandra, "If she is not here, there must be a reason. . . ."

"Don't worry, don't worry. She'll be here. Maybe she's a little late. And even if not—well, we are here," he added in triumph.

Although his words had been encouraging, a shadow of doubt had crossed his mind. From all he had heard of

Theodora's sister, it was impossible to think Aleksandra would not meet two travel-weary relatives upon their arrival at this cold foreign-looking station where—it now made him uneasy to see—there were so many policemen. He gripped their valise more tightly. In Poland, he had learned to fear policemen: they were often not one's own countrymen and they were all the more dangerous because if you were arrested, you might not understand what they asked of you. The only Polish word they seemed to know was "Stop!" But then after you had stopped you had to explain everything, and then the trouble would start. . . .

What's more, he now noted to himself, with a frown, these men did not seem the friendly policemen such as they had met on the Island: these men had their clubs at the ready. Nervously he gripped Theodora's hand, keeping her close by his side; but reluctant to say anything that might frighten her, he said nothing. But for once, Theodora was oblivious: she was intent only on finding her sister.

"I see a telephone there by the door. If she's not here, there must be a reason," she repeated. Maybe she's sick. . . ." Her voice trailed off.

"Maybe she's inside the station. Not everybody is permitted to come running out to greet passengers or send them off. It would be . . . chaos." He had said this to calm her; in fact, he now saw many people assembling on the other side of the track—women and children mostly. But more women than men: America seemed to be a nation of women. He meant to ask Theodora later whether, besides being street car conductors and other unheard of things, women here could also be policemen and soldiers.

He saw now that there was a difference in the men's uniforms: some were indeed policemen, but others were soldiers. The soldiers appeared to be upset with the women and one of them began scolding a woman who was carrying a flag-like banner, while still another ripped an armband from her coat. Theodora at the moment was thinking only of Aleksandra's absence, but nevertheless Czesio's concern was such that he could not help asking her abruptly what it was the armband said that had so angered the militiaman.

Theodora glanced over at the women, some of whom were also wearing armbands. "Don't Be A Scab," she read aloud quickly. But when Czesio asked under his breath what that meant—he was beginning to feel that even in America perhaps it was safer to speak softly so that the police would not hear you—she only shook her head, saying she did not know, and glanced at him with surprise that he should be asking her such questions at a time like this— when they had just arrived in a strange city and Aleksandra was nowhere to be seen. So Czesio, somewhat abashed, did not pursue his question.

Glancing up at the railroad clock, Czesio noted that they were not, after all, so much behind their scheduled arrival time—so either Aleksandra must arrive soon or for some reason she was not coming at all. Theodora, with a worried frown, declared that what she must do now is telephone her sister at the number Aleksandra had given her. But if her sister did not answer, then—she added forlornly —they would perhaps have to get help from some "travellers' aid." Theodora began hurrying toward the telephone she had seen, murmuring—partly to reassure herself, thought Czesio—that telephoning was no problem, that she knew how to do it, and began seeking a few coins in her purse. For the hundredth time, Czesio regretted his ignorance of the language: it was not right, he felt, for a man to have to let his wife take on responsibilities of that nature.

As he waited for Theodora (he could see that she was having some problem—she had already hung up once and dialed again), he began watching the children who were now boarding the train. He realized with a shock of surprise that the women were not, after all, going with the children: that the children were going alone. And such children! exclaimed Czesio to himself as he watched. Over one hundred of them slowly boarding the train in pairs and looking, he thought, like orphans lining up for food. He himself was shivering slightly with the cold as he stood watching, and it struck him that these were the most poorly clad children he had ever seen in his life; not a pair of boots among them, the broken soles of their shoes flapping like crows as they shuffled toward the train. Through the holes in their ragged undershirts Czesio could see the bare skin, pimpled over with cold. And the women—who appeared to be their mothers—were in no better shape than the children: most were without coats or gloves, their hands like knobby red potatoes from the cold. And they too wore those forbidden armbands, and seemed now to be silently defying the police, who had increased in number. Stunned, Czesio saw an officer raise his club to—mother of God!—a woman.
. . . Instinctively, Czesio ran toward them to protest—he was thinking of his mother and sister: even on the manor where the women had sometimes worked, no one had taken a club to beat them. So Czesio cried out "Stop!" but of course it was the wrong language. And now there were not just a few policemen, but an entire army, and the crush of hundreds of women and children all screaming with terror

as the militia, too, arrived from nowhere, from the train itself, it seemed, like a bad genie sprung from the sorcery of the train itself; and the militiamen began flailing about, beating the mothers and yes, Czesio saw now, some fathers too, and tearing the children away from their mothers as if they were being kidnapped, and armed troops were suddenly everywhere in the station, arresting everyone in sight, including himself. As the policeman's club came down upon him, and the officer had begun dragging him away, he could see Theodora's look of horror, could see her rush toward the arresting policeman crying, "Stop! Stop!" and trying with all her strength to pull Czesio from the officer. But, like the claw of a great bear, the officer's club rose in the air, then lashed out at Theodora, striking her on her shoulders, her arms, her hands. Blind with fury, Czesio managed to free himself long enough to push the officer down, away from Theodora, but then another officer came, and another and another, and Czesio was dragged away, under arrest, while Theodora lay groaning on the ground. And Theodora too, he saw, in spite of her injuries, was under arrest as were all the mothers in the station. His head throbbing, and nearly delirious with rage as the officers shoved him into a paddy wagon, Czesio thought he heard the women singing; and as the wagon pulled away from the station, he could hear like a rising wind, the chant of their voices: "Bread and roses . . . bread and roses."

WHEN CZESIO HAD PAID their fine (Henryk had generously wired them a sum that it would take Czesio months to repay), he visited the hospital where Theodora lay, her arm in a heavy cast from her shoulder to her wrist, the broken fingers of her hands held in place by ugly devices that he could not bear to look at.

"Who were they?" asked Czesio hoarsely. "What did they want?"

Theodora looked away. "A fifty-four hour work week. For women and children," she added, and burst into tears. Czesio kissed the cruel cast that imprisoned her arm. His voice broke and it was only with an effort that he kept himself from sobbing aloud: "And now my darling, what is it *you* want? Tell me—I swear to you I will do it, if it means killing that. . . ."

She shook her head sadly. "No. No. Nothing. . . . I want only to leave here. I want only never to see this place again."

So THEY LEFT Lawrence forever, and moved to Detroit, where it was true, as Aleksandra had assured them, it was not hard for Czesio to find work. The world's most modern assembly line awaited him, and Czesio was suddenly as bound to the Ford Motor Company as ever his father had been to the manor. But he made good wages, he said to himself as the shining black Fords moved away from him and into the future, into the world of highways and radios and washing machines and ever more magical typewriters, which Theodora, however, could never master: the little finger of her right had continued to point rigidly into empty space, while the thumb and forefinger remained curved into a stony question mark. Their doctor said that she should, when she felt up to it—perhaps in a year or so— have the bones rebroken and reset; but the children had begun to arrive by then, first the twins and then a girl, and

Theodora said she could not spare the time. "With children," she added wryly, "you need not just one hand, but three. . . ." So they had waited a year, and then another, till Theodora herself had ceased to speak of it, and Czesio felt that, out of respect for her, he should not bring up a subject she seemed to avoid. Yet there were times when, as he watched her awkwardly thread a needle, such remorse would seize him—him her Protector!—that he would want to take his own hand and break it against a wall.

But when, only a few years later, along with thousands of others during the Great War, Theodora died, leaving him with three young orphans, the Funeral Director came to consult with him about arrangements for Theodora. He sought permission, he said, to break the bones of the hand again so that the fingers might lie in dignified tranquillity on the bosom of the deceased—a tradition honored for centuries, the Director said, even on the tombs of kings and queens. Sobbing aloud, Czesio gave his consent. Thus it was, during his lonely vigil at Theodora's wake, Czesio was able to take up the dearly beloved, newly broken hand in his. He kissed it farewell, murmuring, "Ah, it was too good to be true, Theodora. Too good to be true!"

Cousin Ludwika

As the train pulled into the Pittsburgh station, everyone prepared to get off except Alicja. She was suddenly fearful of so final, so irreversible an act. What had she done? She was thousands of miles from her village; she could barely read the signs as the train slowed along the platform, though for the past several months she had been trying to learn English. Glancing out the window at the people who were waiting for the train, she felt shabby and foreign; she should have spent less time on her drawings and thought more about her appearance: she should, at least, have changed from her woolen headscarf to a hat. The men in their bowler hats and the American women standing on the platform with their elegant coats and umbrellas intimidated her: she did not want to get off the train.

But she saw now that a woman was tapping energetically on her dust-filled window: an old woman, with harrowed cheeks and greying hair, a row of tiered wrinkles inscribed on her forehead. Alicja sat back in her seat stunned, unable to smile. *Ah, Ludwika, it cannot be you.* . . . Although it was clear that the woman was smiling at her in recognition, Alicja sat without moving as the scarred and wrinkled hands continued to wave, to tap the window, to knock out their greeting. Then a warm, welcoming smile illumined the devastated face.

"Ludwika—" Alicja managed to say even as, in a rush of grateful tears, she rose from her seat and began running toward the platform to embrace her cousin. Caught up in the shared loss of their village, in the awesome tenderness of women in a foreign land thousands of miles from home, Alicja felt, for the moment, all her fears vanish. She clasped her cousin's scarred hands with their bruised nails in her own—barely refraining from kissing them in apology, thinking: *Imagine, all these years the entire village thought Ludwika was wallowing in luxury in America.*

As THEY STARTED OUT for Ludwika's flat on the North Side, her cousin urged her to raise her long skirts against the mud in the streets: they'd had a flood last year, she explained, that was simply tremendous—the water had reached as high as thirty-six feet. Incredible, it was. And then they'd had more flooding this year, in March and April, her cousin continued—not apologizing, Alicja noticed, for the refuse-littered streets, nor for the long wearying trek back to her flat. Ludwika did insist on carrying Alicja's valise, but when Alicja saw how frequently her cousin paused to catch her breath, she pleaded with her to let her carry her own baggage. It was painfully clear that Ludwika was not well, and Alicja's heart sank with the guilt of adding yet another burden to her cousin's life—particularly as Ludwika was making such an effort to be cheerful as they made their way through the muddy streets to what Ludwika gaily called her "apartment," though it was plain to see that it was nothing but a tenement building.

Alicja had many questions she wanted to ask her cousin, but at the sight of the flat in which Ludwika lived, she knew all her questions would have to wait. . . . She wanted to know about Ludwika's husband, Grzegorz—where was he? She wanted to ask her cousin why she was living in this tenement which seemed to have no windows—ah yes, Alicja saw now that it did have windows: on one side they were covered with a blanket, perhaps to keep out the winter draft, and on the other side Alicja could see the dim reflection of a street lamp. She wanted to ask, above all, how it was that Ludwika Osinka, who had left their village a radiantly happy girl in the bloom of health ("I'm going to America! America!" she had shouted to everyone, triumphantly waving the steamship ticket Grzegorz had sent her), had, in only twelve years, become this old woman with cavernous circles around her dark eyes. She wanted to know where the money she and Grzegorz had earned had gone. Politely she sat down at the little kitchen table with its oilcloth cover and drank tea with lemon out of a glass just as she would have in Lunawicz, and accepted a small piece of honey cake. Ludwika apologized for the cake, confessing with a laugh that she had not baked it herself, she had no time to bake, that in order to be at work by seven, she rose at five; and although she lived on the North Side so that she could be quite close to the factory, she came home too tired to bake—too tired even to eat, she added with a smile.

Alicja nodded: it was painfully clear that Ludwika was much too weary to be sitting at the table with her greenhorn cousin, sipping tea and eating cake, playing hostess to a guest who needed everything. So, in spite of the late hour, Alicja tried to make it clear at once that she did not intend to be a burden on her cousin: she asked hesitantly if

Ludwika had any idea where she, Alicja, might find work. "Even tomorrow, if possible. I don't—"

At the question Ludwika, who had been sitting with her head resting on her hand observing Alicja intently, now sat up and with a flare of energy Alicja would not have thought possible, exclaimed with a hearty laugh: "Oh, don't worry! Don't worry! There's plenty of work for a strong Polish girl. They have Polish girls like us in all the factories here. They love us! They say we never complain. . . . Well, just think of it—they have here the biggest cork factory—the biggest *in the world*—they'd be happy to have you work *there*, Alicja!" Her cousin's voice had taken on a sharp, even taunting edge; the dark eyes glowed. "Would you like to work *there?*" she asked, tilting her head inquiringly toward Alicja.

Alicja, taken aback, frowned at her cousin: the idea repelled her more than she dared say. But fortunately she was not required to answer, for Ludwika continued in the same mocking tone: "Or maybe in a cannery? . . . Girls by the hundreds they need, to peel the fruit, to cut and sort the pickles, to wash the bottles, to put a teeny-tiny piece of pork—" Ludwika measured the piece of pork with a contemptuous gesture of her thumb and forefinger— "into thousands upon thousands of cans of beans. . . ."

"Ludwika, please be serious," Alicja pleaded, beginning to feel deeply offended by Ludwika's tone. "To me . . . it's a matter of life and death. If that's the only work there is for me, very well. And if it pays well—"

Ludwika buried her face in her hands a moment, then nervously smoothed down her hair—not, as Alicja suddenly understood, to make it look better, but as a gesture of concealment, meant to hide Ludwika's feeling of shame that she had such grim news to offer a cousin who had traveled thousands of miles to make a better life for herself. "Alicja, hear me. Such works pays not even a dollar a day. . . . Eighty-five cents now—a couple of years ago it was sixty-five: so you see it's an improvement!" she observed sardonically. "But this is the truth I'm telling you," she added more seriously. "The work is so hard the girls hardly last out two years. They faint—they get sick. I don't work in those places. I work in a nice clean place, not far from here. If it were daylight, you could see it from the window. But anyway, you'll see it, you'll see it. Of course it's not for everybody. . . . It's . . . ," she smiled a long tender smile, as of a woman watching children at play, "it's frightening sometimes. . . .

Alicja tried to imitate her cousin's smile. "But if I can work with you, Ludwika, side by side—"

"No, no. You shouldn't do it. There's something . . . something about it . . . Besides, an artist like you, you need to use your talent. Listen, Alicja, I've talked to a superintendent here. I told him—" Ludwika's exuberance began to return to her at the recollection, "—I told him right off: 'My cousin's a talented artist; she can't be doing your grinding and cutting and burning and polishing. Why, Alicja Osinka can paint like . . . like—' Ludwika laughed. "I can't remember *who* I compared you to—Rembrandt or somebody like that. Anyway, the superintendent wouldn't know the difference who I said . . . I told him: 'You'd be lucky to get someone like her, a girl with such talent.' "

Alicja sat forward eagerly. "And how much—?"

Ludwika shrugged, wrinkled her brow as if at some invisible annoyance, then rubbed her forehead with her bruised fingertips.

81

"It pays according to how good you are. . . . That is to say, how fast you are. It's hard work—it's not like being an educated lady with fancy clothes and your own desk. But I thought you might like it because, after all, you were taking lessons—from Jerzy Gutowski, no? So, you know all about colors and brushes and that kind of thing. I tell you, it's only because I know the superintendent from another place I used to work at and he trusts me that he said, when she comes in, just to walk over and see him— the place is not more than two, three blocks away. . . ."

"And what will I paint? I've had only a few lessons, you know. . . ."

". . . Cream pitchers? . . ." Ludwika's voice rose to a nervous question, as if fearful Alicja would turn away in insult and disappointment. "And glasses," she went on more cheerfully. "Wine glasses, water glasses, fruit glasses, all kinds of glasses—fancy stuff. And each one has to be trimmed—wait, listen to me, you won't believe how it is in America!—trimmed with *gold*. Yes, with real gold, Alicja," she sang out. "So you have to be careful. Not waste a drop. . . . But it's artistic. I mean, in a certain way, though you do have to follow their pattern. They work ten hours, and then towards the end of the month they get really busy, so sometimes you have to work a couple of nights a week besides. But of course, then you make extra. . . . If you're fast, you can make as much as ten dollars a week."

"Ten dollars! Oh, Ludwika!," she cried, rising in her joy to embrace her cousin. "You're an angel!"

When they had prepared themselves to sleep and were resting side by side in Ludwika's wide iron bed, Alicja lay staring up at a greyish water stain on the ceiling. Ludwika lay with her eyes closed, scarcely moving; she seemed almost asleep. In spite of Alicja's resolve not to ask her cousin to tell her anything unless she herself volunteered to do so, she murmured, almost inaudibly, so that if Ludwika were already asleep, she would not be wakened: "Ludwika, where do you go tomorrow? Where do you work?"

Ludwika opened her eyes, then blinked them shut again, like a mischievous doll. "In a casket factory." Then with a smile she admonished, "Now go to sleep, Alicja. I have to be up at five. Tomorrow there'll be evening work. Somebody important has just died, and he'll need the best." Ludwika chuckled under her breath, a low hoarse sound threading her throat. "The very best. . . ." she repeated. Curling up like a child under the blankets, she barely moved the rest of the night.

Alicja's sleep on the other hand was broken: she was still too excited from her long journey to relax. When finally she did fall asleep, she dreamt that Ludwika was shepherding a long line of black boxes, moving them along like a herd of legless animals, silent and obedient, shuffling toward eternity. Without looking inside Alicja knew that in each box lay someone she had loved: her mother and father, lying side by side; her Uncle Wladek who had gone to England and died of pneumonia the following year; her dear old teacher, Jerzy Gutowski; her childhood friend, Zosia Wiletski, who had died suddenly of tetanus; her mother's sister, Aunt Kazia, who had died in childbirth, her infant buried at her side. . . . And after these boxes, came others, not silent, but moaning and plaintive, a straggling column of thousands . . . millions. . . . And as Alicja lay watching, she was seized by a burning revelation: how every leaf and tree had been fashioned from the bones of these loved ones, the very coffins shaped from their consummated flesh.

When she woke to the sound of rattling wheels under

their window Ludwika had already gone. There was a note on the table:

> Eggs in the icebox. Boil
> some and take with. They'll
> give you a half hour to eat,
> probably.   L.

BY THE END of her first day at the glass factory, Alicja understood why no one in the village had heard from Ludwika. Only by multiplying her exhaustion by thousands of days could anyone in their village have understood the changes in Ludwika since they had last seen her. After applying her brush in countless strokes to the polished edges of cream pitchers—stroke after stroke, line after line, curve after curve, until the rounded lip of the cream pitchers began to seem as vast and eternal as the boundless sea, her arms and legs had begun to tremble, and she felt almost too weak to walk down the factory stairs and make her way back to Ludwika's flat. The short distance from the flat to the factory seemed to have become, since she had crossed it early that morning, a wasteland—trash lying in the mud, broken bottles, a dead animal. And even the November wind, though preferable to the fumes of the factory, did not revive her. By the time she had climbed upstairs to Ludwika's third-floor room, she was too tired either to cook or eat but fell into bed like a stone.

She woke to hear Ludwika moving about the room and rose eagerly to greet her—grateful for the company: even while she had lain in a dreamlike stupor she had felt lonely, had felt the looming presence of the factory to which she must return again in the morning. Ludwika, also, was too weary to prepare anything, so they heated some cabbage soup and sat drinking great quantities of tea. When they had spent some time comparing the events of the day— their talk made hesitant and awkward at first by Alicja's reluctance to complain about the work her cousin had found for her—Alicja felt she had found the opportune moment to ask about Grzegorz.

At the sound of Grzegorz's name, Ludwika's harrowed face became transformed: a flush suffused her cheeks; her dark eyes gleamed in the dim light of the kitchen. "At first Grzegorz was wonderful to me!" she exclaimed. "We even got married. . . . But in America, a wedding is not everything. There's still a whole continent, thousands of miles of it, that a man can run away to if he wants to, and after that nobody can find him. And women too," she added with sudden gaiety. "Oh, I could tell you stories of women who got tired of feeding boarders and just packed up and ran off with one of them!" She shrugged, laughing at Alicja's air of surprise. "But poor Grzegorz . . ." she continued, sighing. "When I first came, everything was beautiful for us. We rented a little place on the South Side. I loved our little house on the hillside, though it was no bigger than a box. I kept carnations in the window, I bought nice dresser scarves and antimacassars and doilies and such things from a neighbor lady who made jeans all day on her sewing machine for a living, but who liked to make nice things for herself at night. . . . And I even had a pretty little bird in a cage who used to talk to me. . . . He learned to say, 'Ludwika! Hello, Ludwika!' he'd say . . . though later he learned other, terrible words from Grzegorz. . . .

". . . Because the mill got to Grzegorz in the end. Often

and often, month after month, there'd be accidents—somebody he knew would get killed, a foreigner like himself who couldn't even understand what the foreman was saying: the man would fall into the crucible or get crushed by a piece of steel or maybe just drop dead of heat exhaustion, right then and there while Grzegorz was working alongside him. . . . You didn't have to be a fortune teller to see that this was going to happen to you, tomorrow or the next day. . . . Then, too, the hours they worked—some of the longest workdays in the whole world!—Grzegorz would come home like a dead man, throw himself into bed and wake up only in time to get to the mill, and after five years of it, he got so he hated it, he got so he was drinking a lot: you know the men believe that drinking helps them stand the heat of the furnaces. So Grzegorz drank. . . . Most of the men around him, his friends, they all drank, they said they had to, to keep up with the work. . . ."

Ludwika sighed. "I can't find it in myself to blame poor Grzegorz. He was a very unhappy man. After all, he came here believing in everything, and everything fell to pieces. I tell you," she added, her eyes flashing defensively, "when Grzegorz was not drinking, he was a good man. . . ." To think how happy we were the first year together! Day after day we thought, 'Next month will be better.' We were full of hope. Yes, that was it—we were living on hope. When they were paying a dollar and sixty-five cents a day he would only say, oh many times he said it, as if to himself, 'It's still better than starving in Poland, yes?' But we couldn't get ahead. We couldn't save anything. And besides meat being very dear here, Grzegorz just didn't like the food here no matter how I fixed it. He always said the vegetables had no taste—and it's true isn't it?—they're dry and wilted, even the cabbage. . . . But how could I go find him fresh vegetables like he had on the farm in Poland? Because *that* was the thing he longed for—the land. He wanted a farm—that was all he could think of, buying a farm some day. So we saved every penny. Then he had an accident—not serious—everybody in the mill has accidents. When it's not too bad, when it's 'minor'—that is, if you don't lose a leg or get your eyes burned out—the men say, 'it's all right, it's nothing; they shrug it off. But Grzegorz's 'nothing' got infected, he was laid up for months, and when he went back to the mill, he was changed—he was bitter. He didn't even want after that ever to have children—not *ever*. 'Shall I bring sons in the world to work in hell?' he asked me. . . ." She paused, glancing at Alicja out of the corner of her eye. "Yes, in America, you don't have children if you don't want. . . . And Grzegorz didn't want. . . . What he wanted was freedom, and he couldn't be free, he was a slave. So he drank more and more, and then one night, he beat me. . . . I should have left him, I suppose, right then. But I kept hoping things would get better. I was so worried about him, always thinking: drinking like that, he will surely have a bad accident—then what will I do alone in America? So, finally, I too went to work in the mill. Yes, don't look so surprised, Alicja. They have women there, and they work right alongside the men sometimes. I was an 'opener'—how do you like that?" Ludwika chuckled to herself. "But we didn't open anything! We didn't open jars, we didn't open doors, we didn't open parties with popping champagne bottles. We didn't open windows, even . . . and it was hot as . . . *hell* there, Alicja. What we opened were pieces of hot steel, they weighed about eight pounds, they came out of the fire and we took them and we separated them, we wrestled with them with all our strength, like Jacob with the angel we wrestled with them, we put our knees down on them to hold them steady and we *tore* them apart by the sheer strength of our whole bodies. . . . And we did that for hours and hours until about noon we sat down by the light of the furnace and we ate our lunch. . . ."

Ludwika paused, glancing at Alicja, with a faint, conspiratorial smile as if sharing a secret: ". . . So, finally, a year after Grzegorz took his freedom, I got work in the casket factory. To tell the truth, at first I never thought about the work—I mean, about why there were all these boxes that had to be beautified. I was so young—what did I know about such things, and besides, two girls from the Old Country work with me—Teosia Zdziarski—do you remember her? She used to come from Kolno to Lunawicz sometimes to visit her grandmother?—and Mańka Kaszubski—and we have some pretty good times together, the three of us. . . . You know, you can get positively merry working on caskets—it's like people eating and drinking at a wake. There's Old Mr. Death staring you in the face every minute of the day from seven o'clock in the morning till six at night on a normal day. . . . But there's never a normal day—people don't die 'normally,' they don't die on schedule, so sometimes we work fourteen, fifteen, even eighteen hours. One girl who used to work downstairs—Wanda Juriewicz, I remember her name was—fell down fainting after she'd worked twenty-four hours straight. . . .

"But still, for me, Alicja, it was an improvement at least over the 'opener.' At least I could sit down, which meant a lot to me after being sick that year with typhoid. . . . When I first started, they put me at a table, and—what do you know?—they gave us some glue pots, like we were children in school cutting and pasting from a coloring book.

We'd cover the wooden bars with strips of black silk, first one side, then the other. Most of us on that floor did the same work. But me, after a couple of months I was picked to assemble the bars—the handles for the caskets, you know—and hammer them together. Hammer, hammer, hammer—I almost lost my hearing from the great music I made there on the first floor! But lucky for me they thought I had a future there—a *future*"—Ludwika laughed heartily, her eyes closed momentarily as she savored her joke—"and so they wanted me to learn all the parts of the business. So I worked downstairs for a while doing a little specialty work on the metal bars, painting the silver base over with black paint. . . . And just last year—hear this, Alicja— this is a *promotion*, you understand, and at last I'm going to get a pay raise from five dollars a week to—God only knows how rich I was going to be from all those caskets"—Ludwika doubled over a moment with laughter—" last year they switched me upstairs—to the lacquering room. In the lacquering room, we've got a lot of different beautiful stuff, Alicja, you should see it. Ah, the money that's spent on dead people in America, you wouldn't believe it, all for carrying you from the Parlor to the Palace. . . .

"So where was I? In the lacquering room, I take these metal bars, and I dip them in the lacquer, then I place them in the oven to bake, see—just like they were bread, only much more careful than with bread: nothing should burn, not a fleck of dust should fall on them—as if all the dust of eternity won't soon be falling on them!—so the windows have to be kept closed, no matter what the weather, the windows are kept closed because . . ." Ludwika's voice lowered to a dramatic whisper ". . . *because a single drop of dust will spoil the brass handles*. Ah, they make you clean when you die in America!" She laughed again, and rubbed her hands together nervously. "Tomorrow night, Alicja, I have to work for a very important fellow who's just surrendered his power on earth, and because we were out of stock this morning for the beautiful materials that such an important fellow requires to meet his Maker, I may have to work all night—"

"All night, Ludwika! In such a place? . . . Surrounded by. . . . Aren't you afraid?"

Ludwika pursed her lips as if fear were a flavor that had to be tasted.

"Nyah," she said at last, mocking her own fears. "What's to hurt me there? What hurts is fire, water, air— the fire in the mills, the air from the factories, the water from the rivers. Alicja—you *did* remember to boil the water for the tea like I told you? The water here is not . . . is not . . . clean. Last year, during the big typhoid epidemic, I don't even remember how many caskets we prepared. . . . Altogether it was a big scandal here. A couple of years ago, over five hundred people died of typhoid—imagine! A whole village. Like Lunawicz had disappeared. . . . Then last year, they counted six hundred and twenty-two. . . . I hear there's even going to be what they call a "death line" at Carnegie Institute this month—a long line of silhouettes or paper dolls, I don't know exactly what—shall we go and see it? . . . Just think, Alicja, I could right now be a little paper doll in that exhibit except that for some strange reason I'm still alive—for the time being, at least," she added with a whimsical grimace. ". . . Oh, business was so good last year—the girls downstairs plied their paint as fast as an army pitching camp, while Mańka and Teosia and I worked day and night like bakers, upstairs in the annealing room, shoving the handles into the oven. . . .

". . . And this year too," she added with a strange smile, pointing a slow mock-funeral finger in a downward warning motion, first at herself, then at Alicja, "business has been booming . . . because they haven't really solved the problem yet—can you believe it? So though they just installed that new filtration plant this year, I read in the paper that out of every hundred thousand people living in this great city, 131.5 of us can look forward to enjoying the benefits of our factory!" Ludwika laughed. "I must say, when I read that, their numbers really mixed me up: who's going to be that *half* person who dies? All *our* caskets are for whole, entire persons. . . .

"You know what, Alicja, you have to come and visit us there. Who knows? Maybe you could get used to it. . . . I thought at first: 'Alicja's an artist, she's too sensitive, she'll never be able to stand the—not the *work* exactly, but the *idea* of the work. . . . But listen to me—you'll never make more than a dollar a day at that glass factory, no matter how nicely you paint the gold on the glass, because—you have to understand this much—if you work too fast, they'll just cut the rate. . . . So why don't you come and see what we're doing? Come in the evening when Mańka and Teosia and I are doing overtime for some potentate. After seven, the superintendent is usually 'out to lunch' . . . *I* know what!" Ludwika added excitedly. "We'll have a picnic! You make us some sandwiches, Alicja, and bring us some soda pop and some cookies and some candy bars and dress yourself up like a lady in a French painting, with a picnic basket and all. . . . Mańka and Teosia will just love the idea, you'll see! We'll have a feast!"

"'A feast'? In such a place! How can you think of such a thing?"

"In 'such a place' Alicja, it's just what you have to think of—else you go crazy. . . ."

AFTER TWO MONTHS of stroking gold along the edges of cream pitchers, Alicja began to suffer from headaches, her eyes felt seared by the paint, and her right arm had begun to ache so much she could barely hold the brush. It was as if the gold had entered her veins, and in her dreams at night the faint blue rivulets of her veins swelled to a vermilion blaze, while her whole body burned like autumn leaves. By the end of February, the combination of cold weather and the thousands of strokes, each one as perfect as a human eyelash, had begun to cause such pain and trembling in her fingers that she was wasting the precious gold. . . . She paid out a day's wages to a doctor nearby who could find nothing wrong—perhaps she was tired, she needed a vacation, he said; she wished Ludwika had been with her, her cousin would have laughed in his face. Alicja however, merely flung on her coat and slammed the door as she left.

Ludwika had told her there was always a rush of business toward spring, as if people were so weakened by the long dark winter that they succumbed at the first touch of warm weather: the girls nearly always worked overtime at that time of year. So, in early March, Alicja asked her cousin if she could come by the casket factory some evening, bringing Ludwika her dinner. "We could have that 'feast' you were talking about," she added. "And while I'm there maybe you could show me how to do the work so that when their spring rush starts, they could take me on as an extra hand."

Ludwika cheerfully agreed, reminding her that she should come after seven, when the superintendent would not be there. "He'll be gone at least an hour, and if we're lucky he won't come back at all!"

Alicja spent some of her own money for their dinner, buying items more for color than nourishment—long green scallions with pearly globes, bright yellow slices of cheese, a few ovals of boiled egg, several perky red radishes, curled into fronds and four bottles of Nehi. Pleased with her choices, she covered it all with a white towel and carried it in a basket to the factory.

As she made her way carefully up the stairs to the annealing room where Ludwika worked, she paused a moment at one of the windows in the corridor to watch several girls seated at a table wielding their brushes over strips of black silk: the fumes from the glue were so heavy they seemed to ooze palpably through the tightly shut window. Sickened, Alicja hurried on: she felt she did not want to give up painting gold on glassware only to paint glue on black silk. . . .

"A picnic! A picnic!" Ludwika cried when she saw the basket with its bouquet of green scallions. "Mańka! Teosia! Come see what Alicja has brought us!"

The two girls, who had been dipping casket handles in lacquer in preparation for their annealing in the oven, at once set down their trays and ran to join them. Quickly they turned over a casket, and threw a piece of torn silk over the surface for a tablecloth. Mańka brought out several pieces of cake she had baked for the holidays. Ludwika popped open the fizzing orange soda as if they were bottles of champagne. Then they began telling stories— stories of their lives in Poland, stories of other girls from

Home and how they had come to America and what they had expected to find, about what they had actually found—about their lovers, husbands, sweetheart and fiancés who had loved them or married them or not married them, but instead had betrayed and abandoned them for another woman, or who had begun to drink, or had been converted to another religion, or who had been injured in a steel accident, a mining accident, a construction accident, a railroad accident—and stories of girls they had known who, like them, were from the Old Country, and of the jobs they had had: girls who had worked in the soap factories, Mańka said, and could wrap ten thousand bars of soap in a day, and girls in the molasses factory, where their feet stuck to the floor, so that they made a sucking sound when they walked, and girls Teosia had seen who had worked in a match factory and had had their jaws eaten away by the phosphorous, and girls who worked in the gas mantle factories where the asbestos settled on their arms and shoulders like another skin, and girls who worked as foot press operators and pressed a lever twenty-four thousand times a day, and girls who worked in an incandescent light factory, where they gazed all day through a red glass at a serpentine fire in which they held the wires till they fused like melted flesh in their hands, and girls in the candy factories, in rooms shut tight as tombs because the candy might be spoilt by the smoke-filled air, and girls they knew from Zachowo, Kalisz and Konin, from Lunawicz and Lubstowo who worked in mirror factories where they resembled some alien race from Mars, their faces stained red as blood from the oxide of iron, and girls who worked in the tobacco factories where they became addicted to nicotine, and girls who worked in the pickle factories, where their hands moved faster than light, peeling and slicing and mincing, and stuffing bottles that were as shiny as stars because they had been washed by the washing girls, each one a master-piece of cleanliness. . . .

They had sat like this for over an hour, sharing stories of men and women they had known, when suddenly, as if stirred to homesickness by their rare moment of compan-ionship they began to sing songs from their childhood. Mańka pulled a comb from her pocket, and covering it with a piece of tissue paper, played a bumping polka with a funny buzzing tone that made them all laugh, and Alicja and Ludwika joined hands and danced between the caskets till the sweat beaded their brows and Ludwika suddenly began coughing and panting and holding her chest so that they all stopped, and with solemn frightened looks Mańka and Teosia turned back to their dipping trays. The smell of the annealing ovens again saturated the air and Alicja could scarcely breathe for the fumes. She begged her cousin to let her open a window, if only for a few minutes. But Lud-wika, looking pale and haggard, murmured in a low voice that Alicja scarcely recognized, that it was forbidden, the dust clung to the brass handles, the handles would be ruined. . . . "If you can't stand the fumes, Alicja," her cousin said solemnly, "then you can't work in The Death Factory. . . ."

"Oh god, Ludwika—please don't talk like that. . . ."

"Help me into that casket, Alicja. I want to lie down. That one." Ludwika pointed to the widest and most luxur-ious casket in the annealing room, one with solid brass handles and a lining of pearl-white satin.

Astonished, Alicja took her cousin's hand, drawing up a chair for Ludwika to use as a footstool.

"Now watch me," said Ludwika, and climbing first onto the chair, she slowly eased herself down into the casket. "Ah . . . such comfort . . . " she sighed. "Alicja, come in here with me. We'll have a nap!"

Relieved to see that her cousin appeared to be her old self again, Alicja leaped gaily onto the chair, then lowered herself easily beside her cousin.

"How nicely we fit, we two . . ." observed Ludwika with satisfaction. "Mańka! Teosia!" Ludwika called out. "Light a pair of candles—one at our head and one at the foot, and say a prayer for us, a prayer for the dead. . . ."

After placing the candles at each end as Ludwika had instructed, Mańka and Teosia stood beside the casket, giggling and nearly weeping with laughter. "What shall we do next? What next?" they cried. Inspired by the sight of Alicja and Ludwika in the casket, they began "burying" them. They laid a pair of satin pillows at their head, then covered their small bodies with layer upon layer of black silk, all the while laughing and nearly dancing with joy. "Oh, Ludwika," cried Mańka, doubled over with laughter. "I've never had so much fun in my life. . . ."

Then, following Ludwika's instruction to say a prayer, the girls began to murmur softly in their native tongue. In the deep comfort of the box, lulled by their murmuring voices, Alicja dozed. . . . As from a great distance, she could hear the ruffled sound of hammering from the floor below. The softened blows seemed to thread themselves together, becoming a long cable stretching backward in time to her mother's voice, saying *Are we not comfortable here? Here we may rest.* But her mother's voice faded away, and the hammering was suddenly drowned out by the voice of her father sobbing and crying out, *Here lies my Alicja.*

Wherefore, Lord, hast Thou slain her? But now her father's voice too had faded, becoming abruptly, in an explosive, kaleidoscopic shift, the thundering sound of the superintendent who was saying—

"What are you *doing* there, you crazy girls?"

Alicja sat up in the casket, speechless with terror. But Ludwika merely opened one eye, acknowledging the superintendent. Then to Alicja's amazement, Ludwika smiled gaily at the superintendent.

"We are dying," she said.

"Dying!" roared the superintendent, his eyes ablaze. "You're *dismissed!* All of you!"

"Dismissed," repeated Ludwika dreamily. "Ah—wonderful. . . ." And closing her eyes, she folded her hands, murmuring happily, "Now let us sleep."

Cirikwo: A Gypsy Tale

It was because I wanted to save Bakro that I lied to the Shero-Rom, even though I had taken the most solemn oath a gypsy may take, the *sovwakh grobostyr*: the oath from the grave. I was present at the fight which took place while the caravan was camping in the clay pits at Szczesliwice near Warsaw, and of course I saw very clearly that Bakro had struck Dando a near-fatal blow with a knife: it is strictly forbidden for one gypsy to strike another with a metal object. But I was so desperate to save my lover from the Shero-Rom's judgment of *barey mageripen*, which would have condemned him to isolation from all family and friends, that, while I was lying in the ritual grave prepared for this testimony under oath, I tried to deceive the Shero-Rom.

The *Polska Roma* believe that to take the *sovwakh grobostyr* is a guarantee before the world that the witness will testify truthfully, because anyone who perjures himself while he is lying in his freshly dug grave, wrapped in his "shroud," and with a crucifix on either side of him, will surely incur Divine Retribution.

I must say in defense of my folly that, although I was young and very much in love, I did not come to this daring decision without my mother's counsel. Mura—the gypsy name by which my mother was known—did not of course believe in any of the auguries and fairy tales by means of which she earned her living from the *gadjé* world. But she did believe with her whole heart and soul in the right of the Shero-Rom to punish those who break our gypsy laws. And above all, like all our gypsy mothers, she accepted as absolute truth the prophecies made for a newborn child by its guardian spirits, the *Suwbotara*.

My own guardian spirits had come to Mura's tent, as they always came to a newborn child, on the third night after my birth. Mura said (and I believe her), that the spirits entered her tent veiled in a rainbow mist and whispered to her the prophecies that every mother awaits with hope and fear: for the prophecies of the three sister-spirits never fail to come true. . . . On that night, my guardian spirits told Mura that the newborn infant, Cirikwo (myself), would be a strong, intelligent happy child, with a "gift of many tongues"; that in her girlhood Cirikwo would meet and have great difficulty with a "handsome but erring youth"; and finally—it was this prophecy of the third spirit that frightened my mother beyond reason—that I, Cirikwo, would "perish of an untruth."

Because of this last augury, which my mother believed was now about to be fulfilled, Mura resolved to hide some metal object on my body as I lay in the freshly dug grave. In this way, although I would be obliged to repeat the oath that the Shero-Rom would require of me—"May God strike me dead if what I say is false"—the metal would nullify the effect of the untruth, and I would be saved from the fatal consequences of perjury.

Alas, our plan was discovered—not by the Shero-Rom, who was frail and somewhat short-sighted—but by Dando, who, with the vengeful eye of jealousy, saw that in my long plaited hair Mura had concealed a horseshoe nail. Surely my punishment, the *barey mageripen*, was one of the most severe ever meted out by the *Polska Roma* to a young woman: my mother tore her hair in grief and fell in a faint to the earth.

Because I was now "polluted," I could no longer eat or drink with the other gypsies or with my own family: I was a pariah. Ah, to be alone in one's tent, separated from all one loves is a kind of suffering which perhaps the *gadjé* world could never understand. After the joys of the gypsy road, the shared laughter of the caravan, the music and dancing by the campfires—to be thus isolated from all one's former companions is a kind of damnation. And I do believe to this day that although our Shero-Rom is reputed to be one of the wisest of men, that my punishment was so harsh because Dando was the Shero-Rom's son-in-law, and Dando was in love with me—which he had no right to be, for we gypsies are monogamous and do not countenance adultery (Dando, too, would have been "polluted" had I acceded to his unlawful wishes). But I will never know the truth of that, and it is useless to dwell on it.

I had now lost my gypsy family: what else, I thought, was there to do but leave? So one morning I stole out of my lonely tent, taking with me only my *liwa*, the "papers" required of us everywhere in Poland, and some money I had put aside for a wedding dress. My ambition, above all, was to go to America, because I had heard that in America one is absolutely free to travel—thousands of miles if one wishes—without those *liwa* which are such a bane to our gypsies who often know no language but Romany, which anyway is not written, but only spoken.

But I did not have enough money for a steamship ticket

across the Atlantic and I believed that in Paris, a great and tolerant city, I would be able to practice my fortune-telling until I had saved enough money for my passage to America.

And my decision did indeed prove to be a wise one: my life in those early days in Paris was not altogether difficult—thanks to Mura's having taught me all the arts of fortune-telling from my earliest years. It had been Mura's custom to take me with her everywhere, and one of my earliest memories is of a *gadji* woman's palm extended toward my mother, her hand trembling with eagerness as Mura promised her joy or suffering. By the time I was twelve, Mura had taught me all the skills by which a gypsy woman succeeds at fortune-telling, the most important of which is: to never stop talking. It was as enchanting as a bird chirping beside a waterfall to hear Mura's uninterrupted flow of prophecies and promises—and sometimes even a tale of fairies and wicked witches invented on the spot to charm the listener.

Thus, thanks to these early lessons, I was able to earn an honest living in Paris. I worked very hard—from early morning when the mothers would bring their children to the Jardins de Luxembourg until late in the evening when lovers and tourists would be strolling along the Seine. And I was able to save most of what I earned because I had begun living with a student from England, Hartley Williams, who became my lover. But one evening Hartley and I quarreled bitterly after he accused me of practicing magic. This was of course complete nonsense: I tried to explain to him that I had no power at all beyond that given me by a client's childlike desire to know the unknowable. But I must confess that for many weeks after Hartley and I separated I was deeply depressed at the thought that even an educated man like him—he was studying economics at the Sorbonne—could accuse me of such a thing. Even after I finally came to America, I never wrote to Hartley, though my injured pride would have liked to let him know that I had made my way here at last—just as I had planned to do. . . .

The truth, however, is that I had not planned to leave France as soon as I did. At the time, I felt I needed more money to buy clothes suitable for such a voyage, and also I wanted to complete the English studies I had undertaken. But suddenly, the usually liberal French nation had passed a new law aimed at all of us gypsies who were not French citizens, requiring us to carry an "anthropometric certificate."

I recall clearly every detail of the afternoon on which I learned how this dreadful new law applied to me.

It was a beautiful Sunday afternoon and many Parisian ladies were promenading in the Jardins, dressed in their new spring finery. And I, too, was elegantly dressed with my bright red shawl over one shoulder, a new skirt spangled with brightly colored buttons, and several strands of coppery red beads—all of which I afterwards brought with me here to America. But on that afternoon, my peaceful livelihood in France was destroyed: for it was that day that a gendarme first approached me and demanded to see my *anthropometric certificate* which, he claimed, must contain not only the usual information such as date and place of birth, but also my height, my chest measurements, the size of my head, the length of my right ear, the length of my middle and little fingers, the length of my left foot, and the length of my arm as measured from the elbow to the left middle finger. . . .

Absurd as all this sounded, it was totally successful in its aim: to terrorize us gypsies. From that day forward, I could no longer approach a lady sitting in the Jardins or the Tuileries and offer to tell her fortune without some gendarme appearing at my side demanding to see my "certificate."

But, by the grace of God, these tactics of terror turned out to be my salvation, for they forced me to speed up my departure for America: within months after I left France, the Archduke had been assassinated, the Balkans had exploded, and all Europe seemed intent on killing one another. Quickly I arranged for a first class ticket (I had long ago resolved not to go steerage), and spent all my remaining francs on new clothes so that when I arrived at Ellis Island I might look more like a *gadji*: I had by now learned the bitter lesson that it is a fine thing to look like a gypsy when you are being paid to tell fortunes, but when there is a need to speak to government officials, it is wise to dress like a *gadji*.

At last I was on my way to America: but to which America? I had seen dozens of circulars and posters inviting men of all nationalities to come to America and work in the lumber camps, the mines, or in the fields and factories, but not one that invited a gypsy woman to come and earn her living by fortune-telling. My first choice would have been Louisiana: during my two years in France, I had learned to speak French, and several people had told me New Orleans would be an excellent city for a fortune-teller. But the truth is that I was mortally afraid of the malarial climate of Louisiana, about which I had heard so much; and so, finally, I chose to go to Michigan, where so many of my countrymen lived in Hamtramck, near Detroit.

Thus my long exile seemed to have come to an end when, one sunny morning in June, I arrived at Michigan

Central Station and set out at once for a boarding house to which someone on board ship had directed me, where a number of other Poles were living with a woman who took in lodgers. I had, at first, high hopes of making friends among the people of Hamtramck, but to my disappointment I discovered that my countrymen were friendly when they were anxious to know the future but avoided me as a mediator for the Devil when they saw me in the streets: never once was I invited to their homes except to practice my arts. . . . One woman, after buying some beads from me (during the winter months, when it was too cold to stroll in the streets, I sold earrings or beads to supplement my fortune-telling), threw a hot coal at me from her window to ward off what she believed to be my power to do her harm—exactly as she would have done in a village in the Old Country. And I saw more than once how some fashionable lady, believing herself out of sight, would spit three times on the charm or amulet I had sold her. Alas, like the credulous peasants of my village, even here, the women believed that a pariah like myself, who except for her dog had not a friend in the world, had the power to cause their houses to be invaded by the forces of evil and their families to perish. Because of this fearful power which I was assumed to possess, even their children were forbidden to speak to me, though they would sometimes follow me in the street chanting the old rhyme they had now learned in their new tongue:

> My mother told me I never should
> Go with gypsies in the wood.

Because I was not prospering in Hamtramck so well as I had hoped, it became necessary for me to sell my jewelry and practice my fortune-telling arts in other neighborhoods as well, where I hoped the people would not be so fearful of me. One of my favorite places was at the Eastern Market in Detroit: on Saturday mornings when crowds of people were out shopping, I would rent a stall there and sell my jewelry, or sometimes even paper roses, which were then very popular.

I was standing at my stall arranging my beads and earrings when a tall well-dressed gentleman approached me. I recognized him at once, for he had been pointed out to me several times by the shopkeepers on Hastings Street as the man who owned many of the buildings in that part of the city. Although when he approached me I was not at that moment engaged in fortune-telling—he told me later that he had recognized my trade by my traditional gypsy dress— he asked if I would come to his house the following day to tell his fortune: he said there were things he needed to know, and that perhaps I could help him.

Since I knew that Mr. Wellings—that was his name— was a wealthy man, I decided that this was an opportunity to use the *bengoro*, which I had seen my mother employ so successfully on her wealthiest clients. The *bengoro* can inspire fear and awe among even the most well-educated clients: one look at the little "devil" with orange eyes, its pointed ears protruding from its black head which has emerged so mysteriously from a cracked egg and squatting, as it were, in its oozing yolk, is enough to make elegant ladies faint and complacent gentlemen look pale. With this in mind, I prepared the *bengoro* with great care, and, instead of asking Mr. Wellings to fetch me an egg (as I would have done with a peasant woman), I decided to bring my own, placing it carefully in a small basket along with the *bengoro*.

Mr. Wellings himself opened the door for me—clearly he had been awaiting my arrival—and led me through the widest hallway I had ever seen into what he referred to as his study. There were many lovely paintings on the wall, as well as decorative shields and finely sculptured works of copper: I recognized their workmanship because we gypsies have been coppersmiths for many generations. But more than by any of these art objects I was impressed with a ceramic lizard poised on the mantelpiece, its glazed red body as bright as a cardinal's, and staring out at us with his ruby eyes. This seemed to me a very good omen, for to us gypsies the lizard is a sign of good luck: it is forbidden ever to kill one.

Mr. Wellings, who noticed my pleasure in the lizard, explained to me that he had brought it back with him from Mexico, along with many of the copper sculptures which decorated his study. But Mr. Wellings had not invited me to his home to talk about his Mexican works of art: he politely indicated that I should seat myself next to him in a brocaded green chair lavishly fringed with gold-colored tassels. There was a tiled table beside the chair, in a black and white checkerboard pattern; however, I did not place my basket on the table, but kept it close by, well-covered with my shawl.

I began almost at once to ask him a few questions—about his health, his business, his family. He replied that he was married, but had no children: he added with a heavy sigh that he now believed his wife was betraying him with a lover. He rose—still sighing heavily—and, taking down a photograph from the mantelpiece, handed it to me like a man offering evidence. I looked intently at his wife's portrait for several moments: her face seemed to show the ravages of some long grief or illness; her gaze was one of despair: I could not believe that this grieving woman was betraying her husband. I said nothing, however, that might reveal my impressions; but instead, even as Mr. Wellings was replacing the photograph on the mantelpiece, I quickly cracked the egg I had brought and slipped into it the little "devil" with its knowing eyes, while at the same time I began murmuring a few incantatory phrases to cover my action. Upon the sudden appearance of the *bengoro* in our presence, I warned Mr. Wellings, with well-feigned horror, that a dreadful evil was polluting his house, and that unless he took immediate precautions, ruin would certainly follow.

Having used the *bengoro* with what appeared to be excellent results—Mr. Wellings looked very pale and nervous—I followed up with a palm-reading to reinforce my prophecy. Alas—I told him—his health was soon to become precarious, as was that of his wife. I warned him also that, since speaking to him at the market place yesterday, I had seen a spirit rising in a mist; that this spirit was someone near to him who had died but a few months earlier, but who could not rest: the spirit wished to return—for vengeance, perhaps. I was holding his palm lightly in my own as I murmured my warnings with an occasional professional exclamation of surprise and premonition. When I reached the point at which I would have offered to free his house from the evil which polluted it, I looked up at him. There was a strange expression on his face, and, although I am not a timid woman, my blood turned cold at the look in his eyes. Suddenly, the hand which had lain loosely in mine turned and gripped my wrist in a stunning vise, and he began muttering harsh and filthy words of violence and violation which terrified me.

Ah, what a terrific struggle took place in that gentle-man's study surrounded by his beautiful works of art, with the photograph of his wife gazing down upon us with her resonating sorrow. How I kicked and struggled as we fought and tore at one other like dogs. Then, just as we staggered against the mantelpiece and I thought *Now he will strangle me at last,* I managed to free my right hand long enough to seize the red lizard and strike him such a stunning blow in the face that he released me momentarily, cursing me and holding his bleeding mouth. Then indeed I fled in terror—pursued by what I felt was a man made mad by avenging spirits. Never in all my wanderings had I known such fear: I believed then and I believe now that that man would have found some way to rid himself of my wretched body. . . .

My terror was so great that I cannot to this day recall how I returned to my boarding house. I believe some old farmer on his way to the market, upon seeing my distraught condition, gave me a ride back to Hamtramck. Yet—though in the past I would never forget a face—such was my terror on that day that I can remember nothing of the old man except his look of astonishment at the sight of a woman in gypsy clothes, her face bleeding, her clothes torn, nearly insane with fear, and still clutching in her hand a broken piece of ceramic lizard.

The relief I felt as I came in sight of my boarding house and heard my dog barking with joy at my return was so great that I sank to my knees and kissed the ground, thank-ing God for having saved me from so wretched an end.

But alas, my thanksgiving was premature: the very next day an officer came to the boarding house to arrest me—for after I had fled in terror, Mr. Wellings had immediately called the police, claiming that out of compassion, he had allowed a gypsy woman who was begging and selling worthless trinkets to enter his house so that he might give her some food and a few pennies, but that the ungrateful woman had assaulted him, robbing him of some cash he had in a desk drawer of his study, and then fleeing with a valuable art object.

And Mr. Wellings later repeated these wretched lies before the judge, who, however, had no difficulty at all believing them. But who, alas, believes a gypsy? Even though I was under oath—as sacred to me as one I might have made to the Shero-Rom—the judge did not believe me. It was a clear case of the word of a respectable gentleman against that of a gypsy—a member of that accursed tribe who the *gadjé* believe are pagan and immoral, committing crimes of robbery or worse, without remorse: in his concluding remarks to the judge Mr. Wellings' lawyer suggested that it would be a blessing to the country if all gypsies are deported.

Deported! The very sound of the word terrified me; but thank God I was protected by the laws of my new country, if not by the judge: I had, fortunately, only recently become a citizen of the United States; this fact weighed heavily with the judge and appeared to mitigate my "guilt." He went so far as to remark, in a noticeably softened manner, that since the defendant, Cirikwo Cybulski, seemed to have learned the language of our country with such commendable success, she might also learn to live in the country like a decent woman.

These few kind words, however, did not save me from the verdict. And I cannot describe my despair—my feeling of actual physical disintegration—to find myself locked into a cell: the grating of metal on a prison door is more fearful to a gypsy than a creaking scaffold. In horror, I threw myself against the walls of my cell. I sobbed aloud, calling upon my mother to save me; I cried out to the Shero-Rom that I was not a murderer nor an adulteress, that I had not given false testimony. Above all, I prayed to my guardian spirits to save me. . . .

But after weeks of fruitless prayer I have at last accepted the fact that only the relentless passage of time will save me. So now I lie quietly on my bed at night and watch the clock in the corridor as its hands move inexorably into minutes, hours, days. . . . And I have learned to will myself to dream: that I will soon be free, and that I will then seek out my own, my gypsy tribe, and we will wander the world again in our wagons, pausing only to feast and dance around our campfires—and leaving behind us always our terrifying trail of *shpera*—a broom, a kerchief—on the trees, at the crossroads, so that the *gajé* will not dare to follow us, for fear of our curse.

The Way We Lived Then

L ate that afternoon, instead of feeding the chickens, Krzysztof cautiously made his way up the ladder to the loft in order to see if from the southside window of the barn he could catch sight of his son returning along the railroad track. Since at this time of year it was easier to walk the ties than plow through the April mud, both he and Jasiek usually followed the track to the farm.

After yesterday's Easter celebration, which had coincided with Jasiek's birthday, Krzysztof had given his son permission to stay overnight with the Olitski family: not only did Jasiek appreciate getting accordion lessons from Adam Olitski, but his son also enjoyed the company of the Olitskis' daughter, Olcia, who, though only fifteen, had a tender eye for a boy like Jasiek who had a real future ahead of him. In spite of the burden of payments on the small farm Krzysztof had bought after the accident in the Starkville mine, he had managed to keep his son from working in the mines, stubbornly insisting that Jasiek finish high school so that he could go on to the university in the fall— he meant his son to be an educated man, an engineer perhaps—not a half-crippled miner like himself who had spent the best years of his life scraping coal from a black tomb four miles beneath the earth.

If only Józia had lived to see Jasiek grow up to be this tall, promising young man, things might be different: perhaps she and Krzysztof would have done as they would have in the Old Country; perhaps they would even now be approaching the Olitski family, inviting them to a glass of vodka or brandy, arranging something for the future—a formal betrothal perhaps, that would preserve Olcia for his son, if Jasiek so desired, and yet give the boy some time to think through the seriousness of marriage, with all its responsibilities. But trying to raise his son alone here in America, he hardly knew what was the right thing to do: at eighteen, Jasiek was old enough to get himself into serious trouble, Krzysztof murmured to himself as he raised the window facing the track of the Colorado and Southeastern, and although he liked Olcia well enough—she was an attractive, well-behaved girl who clung to the customs of her parents' country—he was dead set against an early marriage for Jasiek.

But what he hoped for, above all, was for this wretched strike to end, so that a man could at least walk down the road to the store, or pick up the mail at the post office. Instead, for seven months the whole community had known nothing except this state of siege—an entire town evicted from company houses and living in canvas tents. It wasn't that he didn't support the strikers, Krzysztof explained to any invisible critics—after all, it was only by a miracle that he himself had survived his years in the mines—but he was no longer convinced that these bitter struggles were worth what they cost. Just look at what happened in that big strike ten years back: they'd practically kidnapped the leaders of the strike, forcing them into boxcars that were heading out to the prairies of Kansas and the plains of Texas and New Mexico, then shoved them out of the cars into the middle of nowhere—not a farmhouse or a human being to be seen. And of course they'd lost the strike. . . . And this time, the fighting was even worse—the militia sent down to the mining camp, both sides shooting at one another. . . . When Krzysztof and Jósia, along with his brother Juliusz, had fled Poland so that the men might escape military service in Russia, could one ever have imagined, Krzysztof asked himself, shaking his head, that they would see free men fighting the army of the State as fiercely as if they had been invaded by a foreign enemy?

Darkness would not yet have fallen before Jasiek started back this way from the Olitskis', but in these bad times it made him uneasy whenever Jasiek was not busy around the farm, doing the chores Krzysztof hoped would keep his son occupied. He had done everything he could think of to keep Jasiek away from the tent colony—yet only yesterday he himself had felt obliged to attend their Easter party, since the Olitskis had made such a point of its being Jasiek's birthday as well, celebrating it with gifts and a birthday cake Marya Olitski had baked just for him. There had been accordion music and dancing, and right in the midst of the party Jasiek and Olcia had slipped away. One moment Krzysztof had been watching with pleasure as the young couple danced a *mazurka*—Olcia dressed in a Polish peasant costume made by her mother, her long braided hair flying like golden canaries, and Jasiek proudly wearing a long white *capote* just like the one Krzysztof had worn in Lunawicz. And then, to Krzysztof's dismay, the young couple had disappeared together.

Scanning the railroad track, Krzysztof now thought he saw Jasiek, but the April wind momentarily blurred his vision, and when he looked again, the young man, whoever he was, had disappeared in the direction of the arroyo. It was the red bandanna that had confused him. Too often in the past few months, Jasiek, in order to show his sympathy for the Olitski family who were living in the tent colony along with the other miners, would wear the same red kerchief around his neck that nearly all the strikers wore. But to the militiamen sent down from Denver, these kerchiefs were a red flag to a bull, and he had several times asked Jasiek to stop wearing them.

Peering eastward he now saw more red-kerchiefed men, but he could not tell whether they were headed in the direction of his farm or would turn toward the arroyo. He shifted his weight to his stronger leg, and lifted his body half-way out the window so that he could see the outskirts of the tent colony: he saw no one walking about—no men with red bandannas—but he did see a small curl of smoke that seemed to be rising from the outermost edge of the colony. Since there were about one hundred and fifty tents, he was not at all certain whose tent the smoke was coming from, but he guessed that one of the women must have knocked over a cooking stove. Disturbed by the sight, Krzysztof stood brooding over this unwelcome knowledge: it had made good sense for him to stay away from the colony during the strike—but the dangers of fire were something he understood all too well, especially since (as he suspected) there could be secret caches of ammunition stored in the strikers' tents. In spite of his many doubts about the wisdom of the strike, he felt obligated now to let the miners know that one of their tents was smoking. . . .

He made his way down the ladder at a speed which surprised himself, taking each rung as quickly as his bad leg permitted. He had never really regained the use of it after that futile rescue mission in Starkville four years back. . . . But for him to think of that day, of the rescue team's desperate efforts to reach the trapped men, including his brother, was to invite guilt and chaos and a strange trembling of his legs: he warned himself that he needed to stay calm, to conserve his strength—that even if he went straight by the tracks of the Colorado and Southeastern, it was still a good half-mile trek from his farm to tent colony.

As he walked along the track, he continued to scan the horizon for Jasiek, hoping to meet him on the way, reconciled, even, to the idea that Olcia might be with him, so long as they were both safely on the farm. . . . No doubt it was the effect of having watched them dance the *mazurka* yesterday, but he had been haunted by memories of weddings and dances and christenings ever since. What a marriageable *magielon* his son would have been in their native village! How the girls of Lunawicz would have vied for his attention—while here in the mining camp there were altogether hardly fifty Poles, and so few Polish girls that young men had to fight to get a dance with a nice girl from Home. And the truth was, Krzysztof admitted to himself with a sigh, Jasiek was lucky to have found a girl who respected the ways of the Old Country—one who had been taught how to prepare for the holidays the way his mother and his sister Lodzia would have done. . . . For himself, every passing year since leaving Lunawicz made his memories more luminous, gilded like some holy manuscript with homesickness and longing. Easter celebrations, for instance: with what reckless extravagance the Wasidewski family used to welcome the end of winter and the arrival of spring, with his mother preparing *swiecone* and *babas* cakes and, carried away by enthusiasm, sometimes a suckling pig as well, roasted with a fragrant stuffing that filled your head like strong drink when you entered the house from out of the cool April air. . . . And then there were the brilliantly decorated Easter eggs on which Lodzia would lavish weeks of artistry before having them consecrated by Father Pankiewicz. But here in the mining camp, of course, no one had time for such fine things as the holiday egg painting he and his sister had loved so much. Even now, he carried in his pocket a pretty stone he and Juliusz had found one day that had reminded them—almost simultaneously—of that Easter ceremony in their village when the manor owner's wife, Magda Poradziński would divide an egg with the Wasidewskis, giving each of them a piece. And afterwards, his father would kiss the lady's hand. . . .

But yesterday with the Olitskis—what a meager Easter celebration it had been: without the Hallow-fare his mother would have prepared for Holy Saturday; without the eggs that Lodzia always painted Krzysztof's favorite colors— gold and blue, or rose and green; without the villagers beating their pots and pans in joyful celebration; without the young boys parading through the village, their faces comically daubed with black paint; and, above all, without the joyful *dyngus*, that madcap sprinkling of water by the young people on Easter Monday. . . . No, he could not imagine that even Olcia, charmed as she seemed to be by his young Jasiek, would appreciate being merrily sprinkled with water. . . . Ah, now *that* was a game he and Józia had known how to play. It brought tears to his eyes to think how lovely—how *young*—Józia had been that spring day; how Krzysztof had seen her hiding behind a birch tree, how he had seized a watering can used for Magda Poradziński's dahlias; how he had sprinkled his future bride so thoroughly that he could see the rounded breasts beneath her cotton bodice—how she had utterly captured his heart by her delighted laughter. . . . No, no. Not in America: no girl would permit it now. . . . Ah, we knew how to enjoy life, he sighed, we knew how to live then.

Sentimental old fool! Krzysztof chastised himself as his game leg sank for a moment in a still-muddy rut along the railroad track. You'd better forget about all those Old Country ways: here in America, nobody needs sprinklings. . . . His father was right: what people needed most was not Easter eggs or *dyngus* games, but *złotys*. Even here in America people needed plenty of *złotys*—needed them more than ever it often seemed to Krzysztof, to buy potatoes and warm clothes and boots for these Colorado snowstorms. Not just storms they were, but regular blizzards, whose heavy snowfalls and fierce winds had surprised him when they first arrived in Colorado. The snowstorms here were just as bad or worse than the blizzards of Poland: or so it seemed to him now that he had got this game leg and was no longer able to leap through the snowdrifts as he'd done as a young man in Lunawicz. Just this last December, right in the middle of the strike, and only three weeks before Christmas, they'd had here the worst blizzard in thirty years —snow four feet deep, with drifts that nearly buried the tent colony—a storm even worse than the historic Great Blizzard of Lunawicz, one fused for him forever with his escape from the Russian police. . . . A terrified young man he had been, just Jasiek's age, running like a hunted animal while blasts of ice-laden air cut through his lungs, running for sanctuary to his beloved teacher, Father Pan-kiewicz—a man such as he was not likely ever to meet

119

again, Krzysztof considered reverently, one who against all odds had taught him to read and write in his native tongue: and who had been promptly arrested for refusing to tell the police in which direction Krzysztof had fled.

But Krzysztof had not fled. He lay hidden under the potatoes of Father Pankiewicz's storage cellar—a burial mound of potatoes covered securely with layers of burlap. He had lain in this strange underworld of potatoes black and cold as lumps of coal until, after what had seemed hours, the police had gone away with Father Pankiewicz; then he had forced open the wooden cellar door that opened onto a field behind the priest's house, and found himself in a narrow snowbound path—a sheer tunnel with the snow piled so high as to form a secure rampart on either side. He had crawled along this seemingly endless white path until it had come to an abrupt end—after which there had been nowhere else to hide but in the treacherous snow coming down like eternity upon his closed eyes. . . .

When he was rescued by Father Pankiewicz's parishioners, they thought at first that he might lose his legs. (But it had taken, not ice and blizzards and burial among mounds of potatoes to cripple a tough Pole like himself, Krzysztof reflected with pride, but a fiery blast like the end of the world in the Starkville mine, and four days of trying to rescue the trapped miners.)

Three months later, he and Juliusz and Józia had made their way to America, crossing the stormy sea in steerage— a winter crossing it had been—and then, afterwards, crossing nearly an entire continent by train—a journey through Hell, with the train circling and loping and switching and advancing and retreating like a defeated army. But they had arrived in Colorado at last, and Juliusz—unlike himself who had never ceased to long for sunlight and air, and had suffered asthmatic agonies in the darkness of the mine—had not seemed to mind the underground work: it was so important, his brother had said over and over, to send money Home. Mama and Papa will save it for us, you'll see, and buy for us a small farm, and some day we'll all go back Home and raise our own crops, we won't be *komorniki* anymore living on *their* estate, renting *their* huts, humbly accepting a *piece* of egg—here Juliusz had spat contemptuously—from the hand of Milady. . . . *Only a few short years you had, Juliusz, and you sent your money home; you never drank like the others; you were waiting for your Polish maiden to come to you with her still-uncut golden hair, a Polish princess you were waiting for. Now, she will never come. Where are you, Juliusz, since that day? They brought you up in the dead of night, with the first ten; they wouldn't bring up the remains of your bodies except under cover of darkness; they wouldn't let us see you—they were afraid of a riot. All the others, Juliusz, the forty others died later, from the afterdamp, you know, but not you, you went first with the great fiery explosion. The coroner insisted that you should all be buried at once, that the sight of the bodies, of* **you,** *Juliusz, of what* **was** *you, might cause a riot, he said. So where are* **you** *now that they have hidden the remains of your body in Starkville? And you know, Juliusz, it was I who had to write the letter home, to say to our dear mother and father, Your son is dead and the company will pay for his burial, but not one penny more because they say (I wrote, Juliusz, that they* **always** *say) it was because of the miners' own carelessness that the mine exploded. Do you know, Juliusz, that I had to write this letter to them? Do you know now?*

He was still mourning Juliusz, apostrophizing his brother, seeking absolution for his failure to rescue him—though he knew perfectly well that Juliusz's body had not been rescueable but fit only for burning or burial—when, as he approached the pump-house buildings, he heard the unmistakable sound of gunfire, and realized that he could advance no farther; the militia were firing on the tents, and, from a sand cut along the track, he saw now that the miners were firing back. That he, Krzysztof Wasidewski, a refugee from the armies of the Czar might suddenly die in the crossfire of a war between citizens of a free country, struck him for a moment as more absurd than tragic, and he might have sat down on the railroad track like a clown gone mad and waited to see how it would all end, had not this insane impulse been at once followed by the question: *But where was Jasiek?* He had begun to quicken his steps toward the Olitski tent when he heard another volley of shots, and he saw now that women and children were fleeing from the tents and from out of the pump-house buildings; they were running toward the arroyo for protection. At once Krzysztof reversed himself, heading north toward the arroyo so that he might reach the Olitski tent by circling the northern rim of the colony. He was running at a speed he would not have thought possible, stumbling through a gravelly mixture of mud and sand, and he had made what he thought was a successful turn southeast toward the tent colony when he stopped short, stunned by the sounds of women screaming in terror as they ran from the tents. . . . More tents were now igniting and Krzysztof could barely see for the smoke and flames. Then there was another volley of gunfire, and Krzysztof threw himself face down in the mud as bullets shredded the canvas tents. He bided his time, waiting for an opportunity to race across the edge of the field to the Olitski tent, which he could see now— thank God—was not burning. . . .

He was still lying face down in the mud waiting for a pause in the gunfire coming fiercely now from both sides, when, by some miracle, the southbound freight train for Ludlow came thundering through—*right on time, seven-thirty,* thought Krzysztof absurdly—as if the militia and the strikers were not firing at one another, as if there were still Easter dancing and birthday cake to enjoy, and not bullets and flames destroying the tents. . . . Sheltered by the train, he rose from the mud to make an awkward dash across the open field toward the Olitski tent, and had come within twenty feet of their tent when he smelled kerosene: *My god, they are burning down the tents.* . . . At the realization, a wave of nausea doubled him over, and he gagged as he ran. Choking from the smoke-filled air, he staggered into the Olitski tent praying that he would find Jasiek and Olcia hunkered down together, shielding each other. . . . But there was no one—nothing: the tent had been looted, every possession that had belonged to the Olitskis smashed. Marya Olitski's statue of the Madonna of Czestochowa, her head broken into chalky chaos, lay on the floor beside photographs Marya had brought from Poland—one of her parents in wedding dress, standing at an altar while a priest united them forever. But even Forever seemed now to have come to an end: there was no one from the Olitski family here, unless—the idea struck him with blinding clairvoyance—unless they were hidden in a storage pit such as the strikers often dug beneath the floor of their tents.

He had already begun pulling at the splintered edge of the floorboard covering the dirt floor when he heard a roaring wind as loud as an explosion in the mine, and, at the same time, not far from the Olitskis' tent, the sound of babies crying, women screaming, and a single awful cry of pain. . . . At the unearthly sound, Krzysztof felt at once, with a strange and terrible resignation, that it were far better for him to perish now in the Olitskis' tent then ever again to hear such a mournful cry of terror and loss. He staggered, reeling, out of the tent and gazed around him in shock, feeling he must be delirious—the awful cry could not have come from the tents, it must have come from his own head, from his very soul perhaps, which was trying in terror to escape from his body.

And suddenly, Krzysztof now saw with unbelief, the enemy of the strikers had become their friend. Suddenly, the militiamen were carrying babies from out of the flaming tents, they were sheltering the terrified women and children from the conflagration, they were running in a frenzy from tent to tent, they were plunging like heroes or madmen into the crumbling, soaring, flaring flashes of ignited canvas, they were rescuing infants, working like a water brigade, handing out children: Krzysztof saw in amazement one of the strikers' most hated militiamen emerge from a tent with a babe under each arm—heroic, diabolical, a repentant Satan who had gone too far in his work. . . . But even as Krzysztof stood, momentarily transfixed, behind him the Olitski tent had begun to fill with smoke. Krzysztof rushed back in: if there had been women and children hiding from the gunfire in the other tents, if not everyone had fled to the pump-house or the arroyo, might not Jasiek and Olcia too be hiding here somewhere in the tent—if not above ground, then below, buried below in a pit, a cave, an earth-womb where Jasiek and Olcia might have believed themselves safe from the gunfire? Crawling over the broken head of the Madonna and the scattered remains of the Olitskis' worldly goods, he began pulling with all his strength at the wooden floorboard: it seemed to him now something foreordained that, finally, after the long years of slow death deep in the earth, he should be seeking Jasiek too under the earth, just as he had sought Juliusz—terrified of finding him, terrified of not finding him. Struck again with that cold terror of the Starkville mine, he clawed at the floor with his bare hands as if he were clawing again at the coal which had buried Juliusz. But the board did not move, it was hot to his hands, it seemed his fingers would melt from the heat, yet there was not a sound, not a call for help or a knocking answer such as they had listened for from the men in Starkville: for four days they had listened, listened . . . and when they had finally arrived, forty men were dead from the afterdamp. *Jasiek*, he cried, *there is no afterdamp here, there is no afterlife here.* . . . God forgive me, he moaned, as he knelt in the smoking tent to pray, convinced that if there was a pit beneath the tent he could not reach it, that, like the men trapped in the mine, Jasiek would not be rescued in time. He lay himself down on the floor, sobbing, convinced that Jasiek and Olcia lay together like a charred and smoldering log, wound in an eternal embrace never to be loosened in this world or the next. And as he lay sobbing, clinging to the floorboard as to a spar at sea, the pain in his chest grew pitilessly hotter, and, at the same time, colder still than the snowbound tunnel of Lunawicz where he had lain quietly breathing in what he had believed to be his death. This new pain was the bright breath of God entering him at last, relieving him of all the bitter loss that had lain in his heart for years—the loss of Józia, the loss of his parents, the loss of Juliusz, the loss of Lunawicz, the loss of all those years of joy. And, just as he had done in the snow-tunnel, Krzysztof closed his eyes, strangely at peace to be free of all loss except the presence of God.

. . . And here too, just as it had come to pass Lunawicz, he understood after what seemed many hours, that they were rescuing him. . . . He lay listening to Jasiek's voice calling him back to this life, back to all his losses—for his sake, Jasiek was sobbing, for Olcia's sake, for the sake of their child. . . . "Papa! Speak to us! We are safe, do you hear me? We are safe. See, Papa, Olcia, too, is safe. . . . Papa forgive us. . . . We are married before God—do not judge her, Papa. Forgive us, we did not mean to frighten you. Before God Papa. . . ."

Reluctantly, Krzysztof opened his eyes—not to Jasiek, but to the woman who now—before God—was Jasiek's bride. And in his joy and pain, his tears ran freely into the mud on which he lay: for though Jasiek was safe, he understood now, more than ever, that his son's safety was forever conditional, that neither Jasiek nor Olcia nor the child-to-be would ever be safe—not now, and not at the hour of their death.

God's Place

Witold had left his seat just long enough to move his heavy wicker valise to the platform separating the immigrant coach from the first-class passenger train, and, on his way back, he saw in the seat next to his the girl who had leaped into the harbor at Ellis Island, hoping to swim to the Battery and escape deportation. She had been rescued by a passing barge, the doctors had managed to revive her, and, by the time Witold had seen her, she was already sitting up, looking stunned and humiliated, while a crowd of officials and curious immigrants crowded around. There was a large cut on her forehead which had been bleeding profusely, and which later was said to have required twenty-two stitches at the Ellis Island hospital.

Conflicting rumors had quickly circulated among the other immigrants, namely: that she had come from Poland alone, expecting to be welcomed by her fiancé, but when he had seen her, he had rejected her; that she was not from Poland at all, but from some faraway place—Roumania or Spain or even Morocco; that her name was not really Marya Dolenski, as was declared on the ship's manifest list, but that she was some runaway minor from Galicia; that her passport was forged, and that, of course, when the authorities had discovered it, they had denied her entry. One elderly man claimed to have heard that the girl had been married to a Pole who had gone off to Mexico to mine gold, but having discovered that she—Marya—had betrayed him, had divorced her. Everyone agreed, however, that she had arrived in America under suspicion, and that after such an act of desperation, she would surely be deported.

And now here she was. For Witold, this was an intimidating prospect: what does one say to a girl who has nearly drowned herself rather than be deported? *There, there, everything will be all right?* Witold certainly would not have said anything so stupid, but he would have liked to know how she managed to convince the immigration officials that she did have a fiancé waiting for her somewhere in the Far West and was, therefore, not "likely to become a public charge."

As Witold stepped carefully around the valises and boxes that overflowed into the aisle, he was considering what he might say to the girl when the train abruptly lurched forward and Witold found himself leaning over her, his right hand clutching the seat behind her, the other gripping the seat in front. He murmured his apologies, but she merely glanced up with a melancholy air, as if he had somehow created this incident in order to humiliate her further. To prove himself innocent, Witold gazed out the window in perfect silence for an entire hour. But presently, upon reflecting that he and Marya Dolenski—or whoever she was—were likely to spend a good many hours together before they arrived at their destinations, he asked in a neutral tone, as if they were continuing a conversation together:

"And so . . . Where do you go now?"

She did not reply directly, but instead turned back the heavy coat which, in spite of the April heat, she had kept folded on her lap. In clear block letters, the immigration officials had written: BRENHAM, TEXAS.

Witold groaned inwardly; they would be traveling over a thousand miles together: his only rescue from their unrelieved companionship would be at St. Louis where Witold would have a layover before going on a tour of the West, sponsored by the railroad. He tried to put a good face on it, however, feigning surprise and pleasure that they would be traveling companions for so many hours together, adding: "And when you arrive there, will you—?"

She turned away as if she had not heard him. With studied attention, she removed the shawl covering her hair, exposing the ugly scar that now ran from the center of her brow down to her left eye: her hair, which had been shaved away around the wound, was just beginning to grow back in a coarse scraggly line along the brow.

When she had folded the shawl, she raised her eyes to his for the first time. They were, Witold noted, a monochromatic black, with the reflected gleam of small animals in moonlight: he noted, too, that she had had no opportunity to change clothes since her desperate leap. Altogether he found the prospect discouraging: an unhappy girl with unkempt hair and wrinkled clothes was not the sort of company Witold would have chosen for a long journey. But, bowing to necessity, he said in an agreeable tone: "But Texas will be good for you. . . . For me, too. You'll find many Poles there. After all, it's almost sixty years ago already since that first Polish settlement was there. You know —Panna Maria?"

"Ah yes, Panna Maria," she repeated haltingly, as if Polish were not her native tongue. "There was a famine, no? People starving. . . . And they sent away their children.

All alone by ship. They . . . most . . . never saw their children again. But they had no choice, did they? . . ." There was a tremor in her voice, and she drew her heavy coat around her knees as if she were cold. "But you say there's opportunity there . . . that they want us . . . *need* us?" Her voice rose slightly in unbelief.

"Oh, 'opportunity'!" he repeated reassuringly. "Opportunity is everywhere in America! Wait a minute . . ." He reached under his seat where he had stored, along with his lunchbox, a paper bag full of brochures received from railroad agents. There were at least a dozen, but he chose the most alluring in order to encourage her. Feeling rather proud of his quick translation (though he was not certain what a *cornucopia* was), he read the advertisement aloud for her: CALIFORNIA: CORNUCOPIA OF THE WORLD: ROOM FOR MILLIONS OF IMMIGRANTS. A CLIMATE FOR HEALTH AND WEALTH WITHOUT BLIZZARDS.

"There—how do you like that?" he asked with an exaggerated air of conspiracy that he thought might bring a smile to her face.

But she shook her head timidly. "But California is . . . so far . . . And I know no one there—"

"And in Texas you know somebody?"

She glanced out the window, her lips forming a line of silence that warned him away. "And what of those others? . . ." she asked after a moment, pointing to an advertisement for the Far West.

Witold spread the folder out on his lap, pleased to tell her about the railroad's offer that he was taking advantage of. He too, he explained, was on his way to Texas—he had plans for a farm there. But first he planned to take a tour sponsored by the railroad so that he could look around at other places: twice a month a special train left St. Louis with thousands of immigrants who—the railroad hoped— would want to buy land and settle further West. "And they take you to St. Louis for a half-price ticket!" he added jovially. "First St. Louis, then the New World!"

"It sounds good. . . . But maybe there's a fraud?" she added with a worried look. "Maybe you could find yourself lost . . . stranded in some strange place? . . ."

Witold shrugged, remarking that of course, as a girl traveling alone, she would think of such a possibility. But as a man, he said, he was unafraid—he was ready to take a chance: what could they do but abandon him? "Why then," he laughed. "I would simply walk all the way to Texas. . . ."

But he saw that her face clouded over with fear at his words, so Witold added more soberly: "But of course, one must be careful. There was that miserable colony in Arkansas you know. I would never go to Arkansas after what Sienkiewicz wrote. . . ."

She looked at him with such bewilderment that, for Witold, her identity fell again into unrecognizable fragments. Perhaps the rumors of Ellis Island were true after all: he could not believe there was a Pole anywhere who had not read or heard of Sienkiewicz' story of the doomed Polish colony in Arkansas.

"'After Bread'?" he reminded her hopefully, realizing too late that, instead of encouraging her, his tone had become sharply incredulous: her eyes took on the shamed, haunted look he had seen after her rescue from the harbor at Ellis Island.

Sighing, Witold turned away. He felt so irritated at the

thought of spending his first day in America trying to engage in conversation with a frightened, ignorant girl, that he made no further attempt to talk to her, but instead immersed himself in a newspaper or sat from time to time with his eyes closed, dozing. Towards evening, however, when he opened his lunchbox, he relented: silently he moved it toward her so that she would feel free to choose whatever she liked from among the bits of cheese, bread-rolls and *babas* cakes he had bought from a street vendor before boarding the train.

She held her hand diffidently over the box; then, after a moment's hesitation, took the smallest piece of cheese.

"Take . . . take," he urged. As he watched her nibble at the piece of cheese, his heart softened. She must surely be traveling on someone else's passport: she could not be more than sixteen. Witold was about to ask her what town or village in Poland she came from when the train came to an unexpected halt. A few minutes later, a man in a company uniform came on board, calling out in a loud voice as he made his way through the immigrant coach that his coal company was now paying miners $2.80 a ton, unheard of wages being offered only because of the recent coal shortage.

Witold rose from his seat in protest as he saw several young men pick up their bags to follow the recruiter: he wanted to shout out a warning to them. Before leaving Lunawicz he had heard many stories. . . . Men returning from America had warned him to stay out of the mines— that, once lured into underground work, they had been trapped in a web of company stores and company-owned houses, doing work that had left many of them crippled forever. It was because of their warnings that Witold had resolved to buy a few acres as far from the coal mines and steel mills of the East as possible.

"A co do pioruna," cursed Witold under his breath as he watched the new recruits loading their packs on their shoulders and moving quickly along the station platform. The girl looked at him in surprise (whether she was or was not Marya Dolenski, Witold thought grimly, she understood a Polish curse). "You didn't like them?" she asked. "You wouldn't go? . . . I thought: if only I were a man, I would go with them. . . . They will make so much money. . . . A girl, even if she can find work, she will get for a whole week's work what they will get in one day." Enviously, she gazed out the window at the departing men.

"Yes, but you'll live!" exclaimed Witold. "While they soon will be dead! No, no," he said angrily. "Not for three dollars a day do they get me! That's why I'm going to buy my own land. . . ."

For the first time, the girl looked up at him, smiling shyly. "Ah yes," she murmured admiringly. "To own your own land. But a girl alone—how is she to plough a field?"

Witold would have liked to ask her about her fiancé. But, recalling the rumors he had heard, he felt any question about who might be waiting for her in Texas could only add to her humiliation; so instead, he changed the subject, telling her a little about himself in a friendly confidential way meant to inspire trust: about how, after his older brother's death, he had inherited the family farm in Lunawicz, and how his mother had encouraged him to take his inheritance and emigrate to America. He only wished, Witold added sadly, that his mother had lived long enough to see him now—on his way West to buy a farm in America. . . .

133

Marya listened to him with childlike attention, her eyes widening from time to time with sympathy or admiration. Witold himself, as he spoke of his future prospects, felt a surge of confidence: with a contented sigh he put away all his brochures, lowered the window shade on the darkening Pennsylvania countryside, and closed his eyes.

WHEN HE AWOKE, the train was slowing to a lurching stop. He rose to his feet to see if he could find out where, exactly, they were stopping: perhaps it was a station where he could buy some coffee and rolls for breakfast. It was not yet dawn, and, in the grey light, he could see the backs of the passengers covered with shawls or coats or newspapers, like so many cabbages shielded against an early frost. Cucumber peelings, apple cores, and the greasy paper used for hastily wrapped sausage sandwiches littered the floor.

The train now came to a complete halt. Witold raised the window shade: it was growing light. The wooden sign on the station was too far away to see, but he noticed a young couple pushing a child in a wheel chair on the back of which they had written: CAREY OHIO IS GOD'S PLACE. Then another train arrived on a parallel track, blocking his view.

That there should be unscheduled stops and unexplained delays did not surprise Witold: he had been told by returning villagers that the longest possible routes to immigrant destinations were a favorite moneymaking scheme of the railroads. A conductor came through announcing that there would be a short delay because so many trains were arriving from all points, stopping here. . . .

"Here?" exclaimed Witold. "In this village?"

The conductor explained with a tolerant shrug—and a faintly visible smile which he immediately suppressed—that there was a holy shrine in Carey where miracles were taking place—they were "curing the afflicted": that hundreds of people were now on their way there. The pilgrims were getting off at this junction and going the rest of the way on foot. At any rate, he said, it was impossible to proceed at present. Then, noting Witold's exasperated expression, he added: "You can get out and stretch your legs a while. We're not going anywhere yet—not till all these . . . "afflicted ones' get off the other train. . . ."

By this time, Marya had awakened and wanted to know what was wrong, why had they stopped: Witold repeated what the conductor had told him. When she asked if she might go out with him—the air in the train overnight had given her a headache—Witold hesitated a moment, then nodded, moving her valise aside for her so that she could follow him out.

It was a relief to be standing on solid ground, after sitting all night in cramped positions barely able to stretch their feet. From the country hillside came a rush of fragrant April air. No town was visible, neither Carey nor the nearby junction, but Witold could see a long line of visitors, walking or being carried toward the shrine. Then, more pilgrims began to arrive from other trains. He and Marya stood watching, immobilized by surprise. Filing by on crutches, in wheel chairs, and hobbling with canes, were men, women, and children, invalids and cripples and blind persons of every age, their faces—transfigured by hope—strangely white in the early morning light. In the small sanctuary chapel at Lunawicz, Witold had seen paintings of the Lord curing the blind and the halt and raising Lazarus from the dead, but in those paintings only a few adoring persons had filled the canvases. Here, suddenly, there were hundreds . . . perhaps thousands, their faces radiant with hope. Many were weeping in joyful anticipation. They began to sing, the sun had risen. Witold heard someone shout that they should kneel and pray.

Sighing, Witold turned away: he had stopped going to church after his brother's death, and, since then, he had felt the pangs of an impostor whenever he had been obliged—out of respect for his mother or some deceased relative—to attend religious services.

He had turned to go back to the train when suddenly, Marya—overcome by the spectacle—fell to the earth, clutching at her waist and retching. She lay on the ground several moments, pale and trembling. When, finally, Witold helped her to her feet, she seemed too weak to walk alone and clung to him with awkward intimacy as he led her back to their coach.

When she had recovered her composure, she thanked him shyly, then asked with a respectful look, humbly deferring to his opinion: "What do you think? Will they be cured? Is it possible?" Because of her description of herself the evening before as a "girl alone," Witold felt a need for caution, not wanting to become, in spite of himself, both friend and advisor. But as she continued to wait with a childlike expectancy—as if once and for all he would give a reasonable explanation of all these miracles—Witold began to tell her about how he had become an unbeliever.

At his mother's insistence, he had gone nearly two thousand wiorstas to the rim of the Arctic Circle to bring back his brother's body, which—Witold added bitterly as he glanced over Marya's shoulder out the train window—the

Russian military authorities claimed to have found in an irrigation ditch frozen to death after a drunken bout at a tavern. He—Witold—knew for a certainty that his brother Marek never drank; moreover, Marek's body had been so badly beaten that even his mother was unable to determine by his hands and feet whether this was the child she had borne twenty years before.

After a bizarre and exhausting journey back to Poland with Marek's body, there had been a funeral Mass for which the entire village had turned out. . . .

The immigrant train had begun again to move slowly forward—Witold heard the conductor assure someone that, in spite of their delay, they would be in St. Louis the next day.

"Then, after the funeral Mass, on our way to the cemetery, something happened . . . I can't explain. . . ." From his wallet, he took out a photograph of his brother Marek; still young and smiling, a bright future ahead of him. "That was two years ago," he added, handing her the photograph.

He had been following the funeral procession to the cemetery. It was April, and the ground had been wet under their feet. On either side of the path, the wild sunflowers had been in bloom. On several rooftops, the storks had returned for their spring nesting. Suddenly, he had sunk down to the earth and begun to pray, but he felt nothing, believed nothing. . . . "I never saw my brother buried. They carried me home, and when I got up again, I was through with all that. I didn't believe anything anymore."

While he had been speaking, Marya had held Marek's photograph on her lap, as if fearful of touching it. Now, resting it in the palm of her hand, she returned it to him.

Somewhat shaken by his own narrative, Witold returned

his brother's photograph to his wallet. "And you?" he asked, feeling that by listening to his story she had incurred an obligation of mutual trust: that she was in turn obliged to yield up her anonymity. But instead, with a soft smile—as if, Witold reflected moodily, the story of his brother's death had been some reassuring bedtime tale—she drew her coat around her and seemed to sleep.

He turned gloomily toward the window: as far as his eye could see, the pilgrims were walking toward the holy shrine, their suffering repeated again and again as the train moved forward, until the vision had become a commonplace.

When, the following day, they were within a few hours of St. Louis, a young florid-faced conductor came on board and informed them—smiling conspiratorially at Witold—that "at last count" ten thousand people had congregated at Carey to be cured.

WHEN THEY ARRIVED in St. Louis, Witold, glancing at the station clock, saw that Marya still had an hour before departure time, and although he felt he would be glad to be relieved of her melancholy presence, he invited her to have coffee with him. He was determined to be friendly and good-humored, but any sympathy he had felt for her had faded; thus when Marya began unexpectedly to talk about herself, he felt more impatience than interest at her sudden desire to confide in him: his mind was already on his next day's departure for the West. With a painful expression of concern for his reaction, she placed a photograph on the table before them, as if it might offer Witold a more convincing explanation than anything she could say: it was a picture of a child of perhaps two or three, staring out at them with Marya's eyes.

"That was all they found—the people at the foundling hospital."

"The *foundling* hospital? Where? In Warsaw?"

She nodded, drawing the photograph toward her and peering at it as if she were trying to identify a stranger. "I was told later . . . about three or four years later, by a woman working there, that probably I'd been kidnapped by some *tsiganes* who were going through the villages at that time—it was not long after the Insurrection—they were tearing down fences, stealing whatever they could lay their hands on . . . kidnapping children. . . ."

"But you remember *some*thing at least?" asked Witold

She sighed. "Very little. Except that there was a woman. Her hand, I remember . . . holding mine."

" 'A woman,' " he repeated, with veiled skepticism. "Who spoke to you . . . in Polish?"

For the first time in their long journey together, her eyes filled with tears. "I don't remember . . ."

"Well. . . . But you didn't stay there—at the foundling hospital? Not the whole time?" He found himself counting out the years of her childhood as if on some indicting abacus. For a foolish young girl, he felt he needed no sad stories: he had heard them all before from the young men boasting and gossiping in the village square.

"No. A few years only. Maybe five or six. . . . I'm not sure. But a woman who was paid by the hospital for taking in foundlings came from Kovno and took me. I worked for her. A *komornitsa*, you know . . ." Her voice broke, and she waited as if for some response from Witold to this description of herself as an impoverished servant. But Witold

139

merely sat silent and ill-at-ease, feeling that there was something she wanted from him in this last-minute appeal which certainly he could not give.

"And then—maybe it was better for me, though in some ways . . . it was worse—this woman from Kovno, she lent me out to another family. There, I lived better. Instead of wooden clogs, I wore boots, and the family—that is, the woman . . . was very kind. But her husband—" She replaced her coffee cup and sat staring at it while her eyes filled again with tears which she made no effort to conceal. After a long silence during which Witold dared say nothing, she continued: "Then, just last year when I thought I could not bear it any longer, Janek, my fiancé . . . he came there to work. He was their dairy man . . . so we were able to see each other often. Janek said he wanted to go to America, and asked me, would I join him? But he had not enough money for both of us, so he said he would go first, and send for me later. . . . I was so happy. . . ."

Witold would have liked to ask whether Janek had kept his promise, but he warned himself that this was no moment to be imprudent: her answer could only involve him further in her affairs. Far from being moved by her confidences, he was now convinced that she was simply another credulous girl who had been seduced by her lover and then abandoned. He glanced covertly at the station clock, and was attempting to make a few conventional remarks about her arrival in Texas when he was stunned into silence by the abrupt change in her expression. Her gaze had followed his nervous glance at the station clock, and she drew back in her seat at once, as if he had struck her. Witold saw that he had further insulted her by his ill-concealed impatience: he felt, almost, as if he should apologize, but this too struck him as absurd. He avoided her eyes, saying nothing.

Slowly she replaced the photograph and rose to her feet. She picked up her handbag, her heavy coat, and her valise, and without so much as shaking his hand, she turned away —in a great hurry now, he saw, to leave him, to avoid any further humiliation. Witold stood up to watch her as she walked quickly toward the station platform; then, with a sigh of relief, he sat down again and finished his coffee: he would not have wanted to participate in one of those awkward farewells, where one stands on the platform, waving goodbye.

THE FOLLOWING MORNING, he left for his tour of the West, and, in the excitement of travel, Marya's face soon faded from his memory, leaving only an image as clear as a silhouette, of the long slashing scar from her brow to her left eye. During his grand tour of the West, he was filled with joy by what he saw: nothing he was ever afterwards to see in America would appear more wonderful to him than the stone monuments of Utah, the green gorges of Oregon, the rushing rivers of Idaho. He felt he could have bought land and settled down in almost any of the places he saw—in a desert, in a wilderness, on a riverbank—and lived and died there a happy man.

But his destiny was decided, after all, by the resonating music of his own language which lured him to Texas just as he had first planned. While he stood gazing out at the Grand Canyon one afternoon—feeling that this, after all, was what he had been seeking in America, this luxury of boundless space serving no other purpose than to be looked at—he overheard an elderly couple speaking his language. When Witold approached them, greeting them respectfully in their native tongue, he and the Gadomskis became fast friends. They were, they told Witold with pride, descendants of the original immigrants who had settled in Panna Maria: the Gadomski family had later left the Polish colony and had settled in Washington County, not far from Houston. They were now, they said, about to return to their farm, and they offered to take Witold back with them, to live and work on their land until he found a suitable farm of his own.

Witold did not pause to question this stroke of good fortune in America: he followed the Gadomskis back to Texas, and dedicated himself to their farm as if it had been his own—watering their cattle, caring for their crops, mending their oak fences, and, meanwhile, learning all he could about rice and cotton so as to insure a good future for himself.

As the months passed, he thought himself well-pleased in America. The Gadomskis urged him to marry, but, in spite of his frequent loneliness and seasonal nostalgia for Lunawicz, Witold insisted that he was happy as he was; and besides, he joked, there were no pretty girls among their neighbors: perhaps he would go back to Lunawicz one day and get himself a wife. Then one evening, while reading an Austin newspaper, he noticed a photograph of a girl who, he thought, looked very much like Marya Dolenski, though the photograph did not reveal any scar. And again on the following evening, as his cattle dipped their heads into the watering pond, and the Texas sun slanted like an annunciation across the sky, he found himself thinking of Marya, wondering whether, when she had arrived in Brenham, she had found her Janek—or anyone at all—waiting to help her.

On impulse, one weekend while returning from Austin, he decided to stop off at Brenham to make a few inquiries about her—asking shopkeepers and restaurant owners whether they had ever seen or heard of a girl named Marya Dolenski—a girl about sixteen, he said, with dark hair and eyes, and with a long, conspicuous scar from her brow to her left eye. Witold was surprised to find that a clerk in a dry goods shop did indeed remember such a girl, who had arrived in town "about a year or two ago" and then had abruptly disappeared one morning—he thought she had gone off to Mexico. Another man, with whom Witold shared his morning coffee at a highway restaurant and who said he worked at the local hospital, said he had seen a girl there who answered to Witold's description, but had heard that she had died in childbirth. But a woman who happened to overhear their conversation claimed that she had heard that after giving up her child for adoption, the girl had gone to Mexico to join the Revolution there. . . .

Whatever the truth, Marya Dolenski had disappeared and, like the circumstances in which Witold had first seen her, her disappearance was clouded with rumors. Nevertheless, Witold continued to make inquiries now and then, at baptisms or weddings or Polish festivals, but he learned nothing new. Finally, he accepted the fact that Marya had simply vanished: in a nation whose flood of immigrants had only recently slowed down due to the war in Europe, Marya Dolenski had become merely one more anonymous immigrant—whereabouts unknown. As the months passed, he began to believe that the unfortunate girl had died, either at her own hand, or in some tragic circumstance from which no one had thought to rescue her. The conviction that the girl was dead—dead *forever*—he added to himself irrationally, as if some deaths were temporary— filled him with a long-forgotten despair: he began abruptly to feel the same bouts of helpless rage he had experienced at the death of his brother. He found himself quarreling with his neighbors about pasture rights, and with the Mexicans who worked on his farm over what he imagined was their failure to follow instructions. He began to feel that rising at four in the morning to take care of animals was a form of involuntary servitude. He lay in bed listening to the war news on the radio, postponing the harvesting of his crops one fatal season until they had been burned to dust by the hottest year, his neighbors said, since the Civil War. Then one day, just before Easter, he stood by indifferently while his farm was auctioned off to an enterprising young immigrant, after which he moved to Austin, where he rented a room on East Sixth Street. By the time the United States had declared war on Germany, the money he had received for his farm was gone, and he had begun panhandling on the streets of Austin. He began to live in the past, glorifying his memories of Lunawicz—its beautiful belfry which tolled the hours, the splendid autumn harvests, and even the fierce winter blizzards which called upon a man's every resource to survive, but that were always followed by the resurrecting festivals of spring. He found himself thinking more and more of the lost girl, Marya Dolenski, whose memory became blurred with the memory of everything else he had lost somewhere between Ellis Island and the Gulf of Mexico. Then one day, as he was reading the long list of the names of men who had been cut down in the War to End All Wars, he knelt down on the ground and began to pray: God seemed all that was left to him, and he determined on that day to shoulder Him as a visible burden. He nailed together a pair of wooden boards, hoisted them across his shoulders, and began his long penance, proclaiming: AMERICA IS GOD'S PLACE.

Pawel in America

Not everyone on this wretched ship, Pawel reflected, was illiterate. Some, like himself, sat in their steerage bunks writing or reading; and one young artist had even been drawing sketches of the passengers—either for himself or others, intending perhaps to barter them for other, more compelling needs, like food or clothing. Dr. Czarnocki was a tall man, nearly six feet, and when he stood up in the hold, where the ceiling was five feet, he was distinctly uncomfortable. However, by leaning against the metal pipes which separated his two-tiered bunk from the others around him, he was able to get a bird's eye view of the three hundred or so passengers with whom he shared the area below decks. As a physician, his impression was that on the whole the men seemed a healthy bunch. Indeed, only the strongest (or the most daring) would be likely to venture such an ordeal: a train ride of several days and nights, packed in with twenty or thirty others on hard wooden benches; a three-week wait for their steamship at Bremen; and then this perilous voyage. Pawel, at least, had seen the sea before in those now seemingly remote times when his family had had the money to send him to Berlin to study, and he had been able, moreover, to do a little traveling around Europe while a student. But for most of these passengers, he felt certain, it must be their first sight of such an infinite ocean. For the women in particular, he thought, who had never been more than a few miles from their village, the relentless immensity of the sea, the joining of water and sky into a boundless vault and the ship moving, moving forever, it seemed, like a lost planet amid the galaxies—all this, he knew must be terrifying to them. He had seen it in their frightened eyes below deck, and in their prayerful terrors as, during a storm, sea water would leak into the hold from the ventilators.

But even the bravest peasant, Pawel said to himself, might tremble at a trip such as this one had been: storms at sea, an outbreak of dysentery, and a death of one of their own—a child. They had, all of them, already lived through the wretchedness of a burial at sea—which had been all the more anguishing to him as a physician because he felt certain that the filth of the hold had contributed to the child's death. Given any decent sanitary conditions, he had silently fumed, the child would have survived.

But compelled to caution by his forged passport (on the ship's manifest list his occupation was recorded as "farmer"), he had been forced to stand by, silent and helpless, as others had prepared the small body for burial. For the most part, this had been done by some of the women on board while the ship's crew stood aside, diffident and fearful, perhaps, of contagion. It had been the women who had first washed the body, then delicately threaded a comb through the soft hair, so that the child should not go to his Maker with the lice that clung like barnacles to the hair of so many of the other children on board; they had then moistened and smoothed the fragile fronds of hair into a single curve like a small scythe, the color of cornsilk. Finally they had wrapped the bundle—no bigger than one's arm—in a piece of canvas, and, accompanied by the loud cries of the women and the despairing scream of the mother, had dropped the bundle into the sea.

There had been absolute silence as the ship sped away from the first death among them. Even the men had wept, crossing themselves.

As he gazed about him now, leaning on his upper bunk —his companion in the lower bunk having, fortunately, gone up on deck—Pawel took special note of three strong-looking young men (the oldest could not have been more than twenty), who, from their air of fierce fraternity and silent collusion struck Pawel as greatly resembling the returning veterans and prisoners he had at first treated as patients and then become close friends with in Lunawicz. One young man in particular, when he had smiled conspiratorially at Pawel over their mush-like dinner (served up in tin plates), reminded him of Maks Golden. Maks, along with a dozen or so others, had been one of those whom he had cared for while they were boys in grammar school, and who, like so many of that young generation, had grown as if by magic to sudden manhood, and then had been abruptly —disastrously—inducted into harsh miliary service in Russia. When they had returned to Poland after five years of service, Pawel had been shocked to discover that many of these men had not heard a word of Polish—unless it were from some wretched political prisoner whom they might be forced to guard; others—Pawel found—from brutal treatment, from insults, from concerted ridicule because of their pretensions to a Polish culture—had lost their sense of having a country of their own to return to: some few, indeed, had lost even their own identities, and wandered through their village fragmented, depressed, isolated. It had been in order to help these returning veterans or political prisoners, seemingly destroyed by the very strangeness of being in the home they had longed for for so many years, that Dr. Czarnocki had begun—at first informally, and then on a regular basis—to receive several patients in his small office in Kolo, only a few wiorstas from Lunawicz. They had come to be treated for their physical symptoms—broken bones badly set, malnutrition, hands or feet crippled from neglect (or, sometimes, from manacles or chains), ulcerated lesions which the authorities had allowed to fester in prison or barracks. And from caring for their external wounds it had been a natural leap to trying, at least, to care for the still-raw wounds of their minds—to listening, guiding, hoping, and even vicariously sharing with them many of their past ordeals. Part of their communal "treatment" had been the visceral pleasure they had experienced in reading aloud some of the great Polish poets, or, more recently, the work of Sienkiewicz in whose international recognition they all took great pride. Of course they had all known that such "teaching" of their native language was forbidden by law, but since these little meetings seemed somehow to relieve their nightmares—and even their bleeding ulcers—Dr. Czarnocki had felt that he had achieved a kind of psychological therapy which he refused to give up.

But when the police finally came and they had all been arrested as revolutionaries and anarchists, it was Pawel Czarnocki and his friend, Bronís Jankowski, as they all realized, against whom the most severe sentences were likely to be inflicted, not only because Czarnocki had been "teaching" Polish, but because, unfortunately, on that night

Bronís had brought with him a copy of Kropotkin in English, because Bronís was a student of English, having long had the hope of emigrating to America some day. Since this "incendiary" book was undeniably in their possession when the police arrived, both he and Bronís were immediately branded as anarchists.

Bronís, employing the expert knowledge he had acquired in prison, had managed, by having his brother quickly borrow money on all his earthly possessions, to get together enough not only to bribe all the officials involved, but to arrange for forged passports for himself and Pawel: Bronís was to go to Canada, and Pawel to America. Thus Bronís became Stanczk, and Pawel became the farmer, Gabryszak.

WHEN, AFTER NEARLY two weeks at sea, they swept past the Statue of Liberty and the mythical Island was at last in sight, the mark of patient misery melted miraculously away, and the passengers' faces became luminous. There was a sudden silence such as Pawel had heard at the raising of the Host at Mass; the men lifted their children to their shoulders, above the heads of the passengers who crowded together at the rail with that mixture of pride and fear Pawel had grown to recognize—as if having survived the long travail of being born in darkness, they were now to be thrust into the ambiguous world of light.

The silence was broken, suddenly, by the cry of a boy about ten who protested that he could not see the Lady, that he, too, wanted to see—everything; and as the boy pushed himself through a forest of baskets and bulky pillow cases stuffed with talismanic treasures which the passengers hoped might help them in the New World, Pawel heard the boy exclaim, his voice tremulous with excitement (and a touch of fear): "The buildings! The buildings! Look! Will we live in such tall buildings?"

But as they stood gazing joyfully at the buildings built magically twenty, thirty stories in midair, there came an abrupt announcement that threw them all into confusion: it would be impossible for them to disembark that day. As his bad luck would have it, Czarnocki growled to himself, he had arrived during the week of the highest number of immigrants ever recorded. (Was all the world escaping Russian prisons? wondered Pawel grimly.) The immigration officials, as the captain accompanied by an immigration officer now informed them, had been working hard all day processing five thousand new arrivals: they could not possibly finish their work today. What was more, there was no room on the Island for these fourteen hundred more: some few, perhaps, might be permitted to sleep on the Island itself; but most of the ship's passengers would have to remain one more night in steerage. So please, the captain asked, would they mind returning now below deck? Only one more night, he promised, and tomorrow morning they would be the very first to be loaded onto the barges.

There was a great groan of disappointment at the announcement, but their own wretched fourteen hundred began obediently shuffling back to the hold with their bags and baggage. Not everyone had understood the captain's announcement; it was a windy April afternoon, and Pawel, too, had had some difficulty hearing every word. But he was able to grasp the monumental numbers: on that small island had already disembarked five times as many persons as lived in Lunawicz and its neighboring villages: the inhabitants of five Polish villages, in short. Pawel was seized with awe at this Malthusian surge—a miracle of begats and begottens; and still this vast country was not filled up, still this country was sending railroad agents, steamship agents, and even well-paid "runners" to tempt young men into abandoning their half-acres of land for these thousands of as yet unmeasured miles.

Czarnocki did not think of himself as a simple man; he had traveled considerably, even making an extended visit to London. He felt he had some idea of the vastness of cities, but a continent so unpeopled that it could rake in five thousand persons a day like so many *zlotys* on a gambling table and yet never be filled, was a concept almost as difficult to grasp as an infinitely duplicable starlit universe. He shook his head in wonder—for the first time, perhaps, questioning his temerity in coming to such a country: he felt himself suddenly reduced to a cell bubbling in the divine magma. Though he might work himself to the bone, no one here would ever be amazed by his work; and even such small cures as he had managed to achieve with his sick veterans in Poland must seem here a mere statistic, happening every day. . . .

Pawel brooded over this as he and the other unfortunate passengers moved slowly along with their boxes and baggage down to the hold. There was vast consternation among them at this latest trial—and many rumors. Some wondered aloud whether there had been an outbreak of some contagious disease, and whether the entire ship might be quarantined as a result (one passenger said he knew there to be a special hospital for such—an entire island of sequestration, all unto itself). Others, more cynical, thought it some bureaucratic trick: perhaps in the morning they would discover a bribe was all that was necessary. But for all of them, it was perhaps the longest night of their long voyage.

When the next day they finally climbed onto the barges to take them to the Island, Pawel's fellow passengers seemed to him much chastened: their initial rapture had been tempered by their last night of anxiety, and many were too weary even to turn to look at the Battery as they headed for the Island.

Nervously, Pawel fingered the number tag on his lapel—30B. When he had noted in Bremen that his new name—Gabryszak—had been the last one on the page of the ship's manifest list, he had worried in spite of himself, that his position on the list might turn out to be in some way significant—that his being last on the page might, for instance, have some unforseeable consequences if there were again today competition for space on the Island.

But upon the barge's landing, he felt reassured: there was no cause to worry; he was (as yet, at least) nearly invisible among so many hundreds. Blindly, he descended the barge, his valise banging his knee at every step, following the other passengers into a hall as immense as a cathedral. But he had no time to admire the beautiful morning light irradiating the hall; already they were climbing the stairs to be examined by men of his profession. He looked up at them admiringly as he made his way up the stairs, limping slightly from the blow his valise had inflicted upon him as they came off the barge. Although these men did not wear the traditional white coats Pawel knew so well, but rather blue jackets which identified them as examiners for the United States Public Health, they did wear, as Pawel immediately noticed, that consecrated scapula of their profession, a stethoscope around their necks.

As a professional man himself, Pawel—unlike the multitudes around him whose voices echoed with fear and foreboding—did not fear the upcoming examination; he felt rather a sort of intellectual pleasure at the sight of the physicians carrying out their duties. But his keen intellectual interest quickly changed to chagrin when, upon reaching the top of the stairs, his lapel was promptly chalk-marked with a ludicrous-looking "L"—no doubt, he thought, the result of that damned valise. To suggest that he might be suffering from some incapacitating disease merely because he had bumped into his own valise stirred in him a rise of indignation—it was an insult to his years of study. He quickly tamped down his sense of outrage, however, as his group of fellow passengers along with himself, were being successfully put through the required trachoma examination—without further labelling—and had already begun moving along, away from the medical examiners toward The Grand Inquisitor (as Pawel promptly dubbed him, trying to mollify his anger with amused detachment, in an unconvincing effort to assure himself that such a chalk mark was more absurd than serious: he knew himself to be in perfect health after all).

. . . But the questions he was being asked were serious and not at all amusing. He now cursed himself for not having joined with the other passengers whom he had sometimes overheard relentlessly rehearsing among themselves for this expected interrogation. But on board ship he had felt it essential to maintain his role as Pawel Gabryszak, farmer, avoiding even casual conversational exchanges with his fellow sufferers (on one occasion, when Pawel had asked a neighborly looking peasant a friendly question about his well-made *sukmana*, the man had immediately begun addressing Pawel as "*Pan*," recognizing Pawel to be, by his manner as well as by his speech, not a peasant, after all, but a member of the upper class).

Pawel had hoped that since he knew English fairly well, having studied it in medical school, that the interrogation, for him, would feel less threatening (the interpreter, who had realized almost immediately that Pawel could manage alone, had abandoned him to care for more needy immigrants). But, in spite of himself, he felt intimidated by the physical arrangements; he stood before his questioner like a prisoner in the dock, carefully reciting the memorized details of his forged passport: Name, Pawel Gabryszak; Occupation, farmer; Born, Lunawicz, Poland; Age, forty-two. Passport issued, March 10, 1907; height, five feet eleven inches (this, at least, was true); Blonde hair, brown eyes. . . . Pawel's silent rehearsal of these statistics was interrupted by a battery of questions:

"Are you married?"

"Yes, sir." (To a woman named Elzbieta, Pawel reminded himself—should the examiner ask.)

"Do you have a job here in America?"

Pawel shook his head, as he knew he should, adding: "No, I'm going to live with my uncle on his farm."

"Where? Where is your uncle's farm?"

Pawel's answer came readily enough. He knew he could not falsify this issue because, very likely, his destination would be marked on his identification tag. "In Minnesota, sir."

"Have you ever been arrested for moral turpitude?"

This question broke through Pawel's scrupulous calm: he was torn between two equally duplicitous roles—between feigning ignorance of the meaning of these words (it would have been a rare farmer indeed who had the least idea what social evils were implied), and feigning moral indignation at the very idea. Pawel opted for a plea of ignorance, and he was relieved to see, that with an impatient gesture, the official was summoning an interpreter to explain this item of "moral turpitude." The interpreter—scowling, either in suspicion or in embarrassment, Pawel was not certain which—began, haltingly, and with considerable self-consciousness, explaining a few "abnormalities" which Pawel had read about many years ago (actually, Pawel thought, the poor man did his obviously distasteful task quite competently). Pawel feigned shock and disbelief: Could anyone do such things? he wondered aloud. With a sigh of relief (and a quick tap of encouragement—or apology—to Pawel's shoulder) the interpreter returned to more desperate immigrants—among them, Pawel noticed, a woman with eight restless children.

As to whether he was a polygamist, when Pawel was asked the (to him) remarkable question, he allowed himself a somewhat looser rein, and protested warmly: "No, no, never!" He even considered for a moment crossing himself to emphasize his denial, but his own deeply held religious convictions inhibited this abuse of his faith, even at such a moment.

The official smiled. "One wife is enough, eh?" But perhaps having regretted his smile, and determined to reassert once again his professional manner, the official abruptly demanded, in a harsh and suspicious tone: "Are you an anarchist?"

This was the question Pawel had most dreaded, and as he answered it, he tried to endow his voice with all the religious piety (and political innocence) of an old *dzaid* in his village, begging for alms that he might go on holy pilgrimages: "Ah, no. No politics. Never politics. I take care of my farm."

Pawel's fervor seemed to impress the examiner, and the man waved him on at last toward another room. As he moved away—nearly trembling with relief at having correctly answered what was, for him, the most perilous question of all—he heard the voice of the interpreter translating a question for an immigrant: "What have you come to America for?"

As Pawel entered the room indicated to him by the official, he understood that he must now submit himself to still another physical examination. He knew himself not to be the least squeamish about nudity; nevertheless it was only with the greatest effort that he controlled his sense of outrage at the sight of a dozen or so other immigrants in the crowded room, their faces showing various degrees of embarrassment. They scarcely dared look at the doctors for shame, as they lowered their trousers, revealing on their legs and thighs jagged scars from childhood accidents in the fields never before regarded as serious, or exposed their virile mats of pubic hair—now suddenly become objects of suspicion, suspected of harboring some invisible animalcule.

Clearly, it was because of his wretched knee, which had caused him to limp slightly as he climbed the stairs that he was now to be subjected to what seemed (to his relief), a fairly routine process: an application of the stethoscope, several requests to cough and breathe deeply as the physician probed and listened; a tapping of the knees (Pawel resisted the impulse to flinch as the tiny hammer struck). After a few minutes, the physician declared that he had found no indication of physical illness except a rapid pulse. Pawel nodded agreement and relief (one never knew what, under such hurried conditions, a man might believe himself to have discovered), and was about to thank the doctor in his most agreeable manner when he was told that "someone" had decided that Gabryszak would require an intelligence test. And the physician indicated—with something of an amused gleam in his eye, Pawel thought—a partially erased "X" on Pawel's coat sleeve that Pawel had not noticed before (indeed, he half-suspected the present doctor of having scrawled the letter himself, out of sheer mischief or malice).

"What!" exclaimed Pawel with angry disdain—in his outrage forgetting to make his English less correct. "Do they think I'm some kind of mental defective?"

The physician narrowed his eyes. The energy—or the language—with which Pawel had ridiculed the notion seemed to have aroused either his suspicion or his resentment. He was silent a moment, glancing down at the floor. Then he shrugged indifferently. "We send you where they say to send you. Step into the next room, please. . . . No doubt," he added with heavy irony, "you'll be only temporarily detained."

Detained. Here was a nightmare Pawel had not foreseen: the very integrity of his mind questioned as though he were the village idiot. As he pulled his suspenders back over his shoulders, he managed to control his anger—an anger not unmixed with fear—as he asked politely how long he would be detained (if they had subjected him to such a humiliating routine merely because he had bumped himself with his own valise, what—Pawel pondered—might they not do to him if they believed him a mental defective?).

"Depends," retorted the doctor, "on how smart you are!"

Left with this ambiguity, Pawel moved into the detention room, where, at least, he hoped for some quiet moment in which he might consider this new twist of fortune and the strategy that might be needed to untangle it.

But he found himself far from alone. The detainees for that day had produced a bumper crop. There were a number of women with children—several of them weeping openly at the possibility of having to choose between sending a detained child back to the Old Country alone and the remainder of the familiy being allowed to enter the New World. There was an old man sitting by the door, his hands resting on a hand-carved wooden cane—a sight which flooded Pawel with memories: he himself had notched just such a walking stick while in medical school. Standing at the barred window, so close to Pawel who also stood by the window that he might have touched her, and staring out at the New York skyline, was a distraught-looking woman of about forty who—it seemed to Pawel—if she had had any way of leaping out the window, would have risked being broken to pieces below, in a mad attempt to swim toward the tall buildings with their windows shining in the April sunlight. Pawel himself, though he had seen great cities before, was struck with awe at the sight of these buildings reflecting sunlight as though by some supernatural power, and inhabited by a new race of men. And—as if to reinforce this fantasy—while he peered over the woman's shoulder, he could see a dirigible balloon moving slowly before their eyes, passing through the air like a great silver bullet. From a fluttering banner which it carried, Pawel, craning his neck, could almost see the word BUY . . . the rest was lost in the fluttering breeze. Ah, they can live here in the very air, like birds in their nests, he exclaimed to himself, and for some reason the thought intimidated him:

perhaps he, who had performed so brilliantly on his medical examinations what seemed to him only a few years ago would now be found wanting amid this new race. It became, suddenly, even conceivable that he might fail an intelligence test. . . .

But he relaxed the moment they brought him into the small room where he was to be given the test. Indeed, he had a faint sense of déjà vu as the three men asked him—politely enough—to be seated: he felt, rather, as if he were being invited by a few men in his village to a game of cards. One of his examiners was smoking a fine-looking pipe; the other two had removed their jackets and were sitting nonchalantly in their shirt sleeves; from their vests, like heraldic emblems of old, hung golden watch chains.

The examiner with the pipe seemed to be trying to put Pawel at his ease—addressing Pawel as Mr. Gabryszak, explaining that Gabryszak was now going to put together a puzzle, and that he—the pipe smoker—would be timing him. As if to emphasize the importance of the time element, the gentleman placed at his right hand a round silver-plated watch with a second hand.

At the sight of the puzzle, Pawel felt a great surge of relief: he recognized the puzzle, had administered it—or one very similar—to several of his young patients. The puzzle consisted of a number of different shapes, including, among others, a triangle, a rectangle, a rhomboid, and a five-pointed star. But in spite of his relief at the familiarity of the test, he realized, also, the dilemma he was now in: if he put the puzzle together too quickly, his examiners might find him too clever by half for a "mere peasant," and might begin asking more subtle—and probably more revealing—questions; but, if he put the puzzle together too slowly, he might be deported as an idiot altogether too stupid to fend for himself in a great nation that already had the ability to live in the air.

Fortunately for him, as he glanced down at the silver watch, there flashed through his mind an event that had taken place while he had been an intern at the hospital. A girl of thirteen had been violated by several farm hands. That she had been so abused had been definitely confirmed by a physical examination. But whether—because she had a reputation for being not quite normal—she had herself initiated the responses from the farm boys, that remained in doubt. Included among other tests given the girl had been one very like this one, and her performance had so impressed everyone that the verdict had turned in her favor. She had completed the puzzle in less than thirty seconds: obviously, her examiners had judged, she was too intelligent to have invited several farm boys to her father's stable. . . .

Pawel, looking down at the table, tried now to calibrate to the second just how long "Gabryszak" might have taken to put together these childish pieces. The man with the pipe was observing intently every move Pawel made, and Pawel's hand trembled slightly—feigning a second's indecision between the rectangle and the rhomboid—as he laid the last wooden piece into the board.

The gentleman with the stopwatch looked admiringly at Pawel. "Good," he announced. "Very good." And leaning on the table he signed in what seemed to Pawel an exquisite hand the cherished *Admitted* card which allowed Pawel to enter the United States.

Pawel's three examiners—looking bored and weary now, as if troubled by this waste of their time—pointed toward the exit; and without remembering to say thank you, Pawel hastened to the door.

But in his excitement at having in his hand at last the coveted entry permission, he took a wrong turn, and found himself wandering about a largely deserted area through which clearly it had not been the examiners' intention to send him. If they were now to find him wandering around, he might be at once considered guilty of something—only God knew what. Nevertheless, he stood still a moment, torn between his dread of being discovered there and his professional curiosity: for he had caught sight of the ever-familiar infirmary stretchers, propped here against the wall, with their thin grey cotton blankets so often used to separate the dead from the dying in crowded clinics. The oppressive stillness of the place told him the rest. Yet what surprised Pawel, even more than to have stumbled in this way upon the morgue, was his own sense of shock: what, after all, had he imagined—that no one would die at the very gate?

Although he felt certain that he was in the morgue, his instinct was to confirm this impression: in spite of his anxiety that he might be discovered, he stepped further into the room to examine it. Built into the wall were eight small doors, rather like ice chests: with a single movement of his hand he might doubtless have confirmed his belief that within those ice chests lay the cadavers of the least-blessed of the arriving immigrants. But as—with a rush of daring—he was about to do so, he heard a scraping of wheels on the floor, the crashing sound of a door, and an attendant began rolling into the morgue an altogether too-familiar sight—a body rolled like a bolt of cloth at the drapers, about to be rammed into the waiting ice chest.

Before the attendant had time to recover from the surprise of finding an immigrant in an area so clearly not permitted to him, Pawel began bowing and waving his *Admitted* card while addressing the attendant in his native tongue as if English were the murkiest of mysteries to him—and so—how was he to have known where to go?

The attendant, far from being annoyed, however, by Pawel's presence, was most sympathetic. He nodded again, and again, as if he understood Pawel's apologies perfectly, and even held the door open for Pawel, pointing with his outstretched arm the direction Pawel was to take. "Go straight ahead. You understand? Don't turn. Just straight ahead."

With expressions of unfeigned gratitude—in Polish— Pawel followed his instructions and went straight ahead. Determined to take no more chances, he scrutinized every posted sign until he found what he needed. RAILROAD TICKETS TO ALL POINTS. He took out his new American dollars—the money changers had short-changed him somewhat, but, fearful of attracting attention, Pawel had pretended not to notice—and examined the signboard for ticket prices. The difference in fares between where he would have liked to be going—to a city like Cleveland or Pittsburgh—and to where Bronís was expecting him—Hibbings, Minnesota—gave Pawel an awesome sense of the distance he had yet to travel in order to meet his old friend. But it was not just the distance that gave him pause. Choosing between an isolated farm in Minnesota and an industrial population like Pittsburgh had been, for him—in his perilous new identity—a choice between the garrote and the gun: in either place it would be impossible for him to practice medicine. Dr. Pawel Czarnocki no longer existed; only the farmer, Gabryszak, had survived. In a large city like Pittsburgh, he might, it was true, be more anonymous: he might shackle himself to some iron-smelting crucible or dig in the anthracite coal fields side by side with the strongest of his own people blindered like mules lest they long for freedom and the sun. But, although a trained physician, for fear of appearing too knowledgeable, he might have been compelled to stand uselessly by while his countrymen perished around him—crushed or burned or cracked apart like overheated glass. He knew he would not have been able to bear it.

On the other hand—a point Bronís seemed not to have considered—becoming a farmer in Minnesota might be equally dangerous for him: he knew virtually nothing about farming, while any ordinary peasant he might meet in Minnesota would know almost everything. Standing in line at the ticket window, as he fingered his new American money, Pawel felt at that moment that he might have tossed a coin to decide his life—so intense was his need to be of some use: even the rumor he had heard on board ship that there was at this very moment a typhoid epidemic in Pittsburgh had seemed to him only one more reason for not being a "farmer" in Minnesota. Nevertheless—and with a sense of self-betrayal—he placed his money at the ticket seller's window and asked for a ticket to Minnesota.

"There's a layover at Chicago," said the ticket seller. "You change trains there—don't forget."

As there would be a short wait before the departure of the special immigrant train heading west, he decided he had better eat now, before boarding. Although the clerk at the ticket window had told him that there would be a dining car (a rare offering for an immigrant train), because they had decided to add a first class coach to the two immigrant coaches, Pawel knew he would not be able to afford to eat in the dining car; so he approached a delicatessen counter where he had seen a blackboard with a big chalked sign offering coffee for three cents. He was tempted to buy several cheese sandwiches, one to eat right away, for, without letting himself think too much about it, he knew himself to have been badly nourished for several weeks now; but at fourteen cents a sandwich (and the cheese sandwiches looked paper thin, with that machine-sliced bread he saw piled up beside the cheese like slabs of slate), he felt he could afford only two sandwiches. And before he had had time to remember to muddle his language a little, he had asked the clerk in his best and most polite English to wrap one of the sandwiches "to go." The counterman looked up in surprise at Pawel's polite but confident tone, and Pawel warned himself he must be more careful: Gabryszak had not learned such grace notes tilling the soil.

As Pawel boarded the train, he was still brooding over what suddenly seemed to him, in his long hegira, his worst problem: how to hide an education that had cost him so many years to acquire. It was a problem which made him feel more lonely and isolated than ever, for it separated him even from his own countrymen in exile, whose greatest ambition must be, he thought ruefully, to master English and to look—and sound—like an American.

He began methodically making his way through the two immigrant coaches until he found an empty seat, and was arranging his few belongings around his feet when he became aware that an old man seated just across from him was expostulating anxiously with the conductor in Polish. Again and again the old man pointed to a card on his coat which said "To the Conductor: Please show the bearer where to change trains and where to get off, as this person does not speak English. Bearer is bound to Spokane, Washington."

The conductor—who saw that Pawel was observing them —gave Pawel a good-natured, collusive wink (for which Pawel would cheerfully have kicked him), assuring the old man in a loud voice, "Yes, yes—you'll get there. Don't worry. You'll all get there—you're all going more or less in the same direction."

Yes, thought Pawel scornfully, *"more or less."* . . . He wanted to say something to the old man, but he did not dare speak a word until the conductor had disappeared down the aisle. Then he leaned over toward him—keeping his voice as low as possible, hoping to alert him to the need for discretion—and murmured a respectful greeting in his native tongue. Pawel's own eyes blurred with tears as he saw the old man's gaze widened, how he positively trembled with pleasure at Pawel's few traditional words of respectful greeting. But after a gasp of recognition, the old man— taking Pawel's cue—merely murmured as softly as a child saying his prayers, "World without end. Amen," and fell asleep.

But the old man was clearly not the only other passenger on the train who spoke Polish: sounds of his native tongue fell through the immigrant train like a morning rain. As they passed mile after mile of the seemingly endless land, the sounds became louder—cries of delight or dismay, of pride or admiration—and sometimes an angry argument. . . . Among all these voices and over the constant sound of the locomotive, Pawel became aware of two men speaking together across the aisle. One, who appeared to be Polish, was speaking English with a prideful emphasis on certain Americanisms, intended, perhaps to show his listener that he was at ease in the new language; the other, he had gathered from their conversation, claimed to be an American who had returned, briefly, to Poland to attend the funeral of a relative. Although the American spoke perfect English, there was, nevertheless a trace of the Old Country in his speech. For both men it was obvious from their conversation that this was not their first voyage from Europe, nor their first on the westward-bound trains. Pawel was eager to hear what they were saying—he felt himself sorely in need of information from whatever source—and he rose from his seat at the window as if to stretch his legs a little by walking up and down in the aisle. In this way, he was able to get a better view of the two men without appearing to be deliberately eavesdropping.

One was a light-haired husky young man of perhaps thirty, with a bright, intelligent face, but with a skin that looked as if it had been burned with a hot poker many times over—it was pitted with scars surrounded by patchy whiteness: the whole of his face seemed to be trying desperately to overcome these previous burns by growing, here and there, a layer of new skin while peeling off the old lacerated skin. He was well-dressed, however, in a tailored suit; Pawel could see pearl cuff-links at his wrists, and at his neck he wore a stiff white collar. In the left hand pocket of his suit, he carried several pencils and a gleaming fountain pen, which he had taken out and was now showing with pride to the man beside him:

"They make me a boss. This is how I do my work now. No more pouring two hundred pounds hot iron for the mold. . . . At first, they offer me two hundred dollars compensation for this. . . ." He waved his hand at his face, but with an air of dismissal that warned the observer not to look too closely.

The elderly man beside him—he was perhaps fifty, with greying hair—shook his head, whether in sympathy or disbelief, Pawel could not tell. He had evidently noticed that Pawel was listening and he nodded and smiled at Pawel in a friendly way, as if inviting him to introduce himself and join their conversation.

Pawel hesitated, however, preferring to stand and listen to the former steel worker who referred to himself as Stefan Maleski.

"I almost die," continued Stefan solemnly. "The boy with me—they never find him. He's melted like iron. Disappeared. He's like nothing but fire—like a thousand years in Hell, no? But I fool everybody. I'm living—" he pounded his leg emphatically "—but only I can't stand up so good anymore. I have an American friend, he tell me, 'Maleski, you get a lawyer.' But I will tell you this, Ludwik," he said, leaning confidentially toward the man next to him, "the company, they don't like lawyers. So they give me this new job. Clean work . . . better pay. . . ."

The older man smiled faintly, as if he knew very well how these things were arranged.

"And you know how much they give that family" continued Maleski, his voice now recklessly loud with indignation. "For this boy, theirs, that burn up like smoke? Two hundred dollars. . . ."

His listener frowned with annoyance at this and looked out the window as if to consider his reply. "I have heard," he said with noticeable coolness, "that they pay the bereaved family as much as two thousand dollars."

Maleski stared at Ludwik a moment in dismay, and looked up at Pawel as if looking for his assistance as a credible witness to contradict this stranger who seemed to be doubting his veracity.

"No, no, no," protested Maleski. "They've got a law—

you listen to me, I been working this country ten years already—I know something about law. There's no Czar here, but they got *law!*" He laughed at his own little joke, but as Ludwik seemed not to appreciate it, he continued, addressing himself now as much to Pawel who stood nearby, as to the elderly man beside him: "Let's say you got killed by a big machine, maybe in Pennsylvania—or Kansas—" he winked now at Pawel as if this macabre idea were merely a violent joke they could all laugh at—"and your *family* still live in the Old Country; then the *law* says the company don't need to pay more than three hundred dollars. . . . In Kansas, is more. Is seven hundred and fifty dollars. Only the real *here*-born Americans get that kind of money you tell me about—two thousand dollars. You say you American, Ludwik?" He grinned with a kind of gleeful malice at Ludwik. "OK. You get killed—you worth more 'n me!"

His two listeners could not help smiling at Maleski's sardonic manner, and the older man now politely asked Pawel where he was going.

"Well . . . first, Chicago. . . ." answered Pawel as ambiguously as he could.

Maleski pointed his elbow in Ludwik's direction. "This guy too—he's going to Chicago. Ludwik, tell this *pan* about Chicago. You can see he's a greenhorn." he laughed amiably.

But Pawel did not smile. It seemed to him that the older man was scrutinizing him, and Pawel was already regretting having joined the two men. He had heard that plainclothes officials sometimes traveled the immigrant trains, ostensibly in order to protect unescorted women from being lured (or abducted) into "white slavery"—but Pawel had learned too well the lesson that police sent out to protect one segment of the population could be used to persecute another segment. . . .

"From what place—did you say you came from Poznan?" asked the elderly man, his blue, inquisitive eyes meeting Pawel's.

Pawel, however, was well aware that he had not mentioned his homeland, and began angrily berating himself for having been tempted into this conversation with a pair of strangers. He tried, therefore, to shift the attention from himself, mentioning, admiringly, that he had noticed Maleski showing his neighbor a fine-looking fountain pen: might he be permitted to see it?

With pride, Maleski took the pen out again, and taking a small notebook from his pocket as well, scrawled the words *American Foundry*, and then with a flourish signed his name, Stefan Z. Maleski.

"Ah . . ." said Pawel with an admiring smile. "You write beautiful English"—remembering just in time *not* to read the words aloud, but to wait for Maleski to read it to him: which Maleski did, adding with pride, "That's my company! That's my name!"

"And so . . . you are a farmer . . . ," observed Ludwik in a conversational tone.

But Pawel had become aware as he held the fountain pen —too expertly, alas, for an illiterate peasant—that the grey-haired gentleman was looking closely at his hands. Quickly Pawel returned the pen to Maleski—managing to resist the strong urge to hide his hands away in his pockets—and, excusing himself, moved quickly away from the men and headed for the dining car, where, he felt, they were not likely to join him.

He knew he could not afford to eat in the dining car;

but, fortunately, it was an early hour of the day and—a Negro waiter immediately informed him—dinner was not being served at that time: there would be a gong sounded through the aisles, he explained, when dinner was served. Pawel, however, pretended he did not understand the waiter, and, with a faint groan, he quickly slid into a seat near the window, holding his head as if he were in intense pain.

Apparently his little pantomime was successful, for when, looking up into the black man's eyes, he asked in a pleading tone—"coffee—only coffee," the man gave him a sympathetic glance and at once brought him hot coffee in a pewter carafe, with cream in a small pitcher. Although he could ill afford it, Pawel placed a half-dollar on the table, murmuring his gratitude with an audible sigh of relief.

While the Negro waiters bustled back and forth, shaking white tablecloths and polishing each piece of silverware before setting it down on the tables, Pawel sat looking out the window. As he watched the landscape appear and disappear for mile after endless mile, he considered, with a faltering heart, the hundreds of miles he had yet to travel before joining Bronís in Minnesota. And he acknowledged to himself that he had come to a land so utterly vast that though it might be true that his identity would never be known, it might also be true that he would never know anyone. Holding his head in his hands, as if truly it had begun to ache, he gazed out the window at the landscape being ruthlessly devoured by a powerful machine that seemed prepared to go on forever, hurling itself through space as if through eons of time, through the very millennia of Evolution itself, but infinitely accelerated, changing mind and matter with such terrifying swiftness that one had no moment, even, to recognize that one had become a new species. The sense of acceleration seemed to throw Pawel's very identity into some remorseless vortex where Dr. Czarnocki, having once plunged, would be lost forever. . . .

He continued to sit, while the coffee grew cold and the waiters murmured among themselves, sat watching as town after town passed before him—small towns filled with hundreds of people—mere villages, some of them—towns where everyone knew who, upon rising, would tomorrow be their friend, who their enemy; towns where they knew their baker or their grocer by name; whose inhabitants knew what school their child would trudge to and what teacher their child loved, and who knew—perhaps above all, thought Pawel—why, if there were a war, they would need to fight: to protect this vastness that was like eternity, these fields of newly planted corn, these apple trees, these churches and stables and barns bigger than houses. . . . And Pawel recalled with anguish how, in Lunawicz, a poor farmer might bring his animals into the cottage to sleep—or the children, if they were too numerous for the cottage, might sleep in the stable with the animals. But at the same time that he felt a mysterious awe at the great country he was about to inherit, he felt a rush of wrath: for here he was, amid this wondrous plenty, his tongue hobbled by the iron clamp of self-betrayal, his years of learning wrenched from him like a broken arm, dangling and useless, his very vigor of mind a handicap.

And as he sat holding his head, he wept for the first time since leaving Lunawicz—from homesickness, from a longing for a loving hand to touch his own, for his lost dream of becoming a truly great physician. Why, this Punch and Judy puppet erstwhile called Czarnocki, he thought with passionate contempt, this croaking ruminant in a peasant's guise, this mumbling mime pretending to chew his language like a giraffe, this *Gabryszak,* had dreamed of becoming a psychiatrist one day, practicing the new healing sciences of the mind. . . .

As he wept, Pawel gradually became aware that his grief had not gone unnoticed—that the Negro waiter was watching him, his eyes filled with pity. Embarrassed, Pawel rose to his feet as if to leave the dining car.

The waiter turned away as if he had seen nothing.

IN THE CHICAGO train station, Pawel experienced a moment's indecision. By prior arrangement, he had paid an extra fourteen dollars for the fare between Chicago and Duluth. But Bronís had told him that Chicago was a very great city, and if Pawel could possibly afford to stay over one night, it would be a good idea—especially if Pawel were to visit a few places which from their point of view as political exiles might be helpful to them at some time in the future.

Upon making a few inquiries, Pawel was assured that there would be no trouble involved: the worst that could happen was that, if for any reason his purchased ticket were not to be honored, "since after all"—the clerk at the window informed him—"an immigrant train is just that, and not a first-class ticket to Anywhere," then Pawel could simply buy another ticket to his destination.

As Pawel was leaving the station, he noticed in the distance the elderly man who had been talking to Maleski, now carrying a heavy brown valise and talking to a porter who took his bag. Pawel swerved abruptly to avoid a direct encounter with the clever Ludwik whose bright questioning blue eyes he recalled all too well; but while he walked as rapidly as he could to an exit, he seemed to see a long grey vista of such avoided encounters stretching out before him: a lifelong exclusion from the company of the educated and the too sharply intelligent.

He continued on his way without stopping, walking all the way from the Wabash Avenue station until he arrived at a small, newly constructed hotel on Clark Street, where, after a brief rest, he sent a telegram to Bronís: LAYOVER IN CHICAGO. ARRIVING HIBBINGS TUESDAY. Then, since it was too early for him to sleep, he began to stroll through the city streets.

He was surprised to discover that he was not pleased with Chicago, although from all he had heard of it, it was supposed to be one of the most progressive, energetic cities in America. But perhaps, he thought, he had taken a wrong turn, for, instead of fine shops and furred ladies, he found himself on the West Side where every second establishment appeared to be a saloon. And the working people he saw on Canal Street appeared just as forlorn and tired as working people everywhere. When he passed what he thought from its nauseating smell must be a soap factory, he began to regret the extra money he was spending on this layover. But Bronís had told him there was actually a so-called "Freethinkers Club" on Halstead Street here, and since (he considered with a wry grimace) in the small town of Hibbings he was going to, such a club could be the last such association of men he might see for a long time, he felt perhaps he should look into it. So, having consulted his small city map to get his bearings again, he began to make his way toward Halstead Street—not strolling now, but walking quickly to make up for lost time.

As he was hurrying through the unfamiliar streets, he

passed a theater billboard offering a performance by E. H. Southern in *Crime and Punishment*. He stopped short as the sight of the billboard struck him with the stunning shock of pleasurable recognition: gone was his dismay at the ever-present saloons, his nausea at the smell of the soap factory; he felt himself transfixed by delight that such an event still existed for the world of the mind. His delight, however, was followed as quickly by a rush of despair: what would he not give for the freedom to sit for several hours in a softly lit theater, surrounded by an audience, many of whom, doubtless, would have read the author's great work? But it was sheer folly for him—for Gabryszak, whose father had perhaps ploughed his fields with a harrow—to stand in the street brooding over theater advertisements: it would have been more appropriate for him to be standing amid the sawdust covered planks of a saloon, listening to talk of fodder and fertilizer. With a heavy sigh of renunciation, Pawel buttoned his long coat against the strong wind coming off the lake, and, moving rapidly through a crowd of working people on their lunch break, he quickly reached the Halstead Street address Bronís had given him.

Here he entered a large saloon, to the rear of which he found, just as Bronís had said he would find, a group of men sitting around, looking at newspapers and talking among themselves.

To avoid being conspicuous, Pawel sat down quickly and ordered a beer; then he looked around him with immense gratification, pleased that he had so successfully followed Bronís' suggestion. What gave him the deepest pleasure was that the men seemed as much at ease as if they were in their own homes. They spoke openly, as if they feared no one. They did not lower their voices; they did not look at him, a sudden stranger in their midst, with suspicion. Their easy freedom filled Pawel with an unprecedented elation: it seemed to him the most impressive thing he had seen in this new country.

There were many foreign language newspapers in the room, but as he saw none close at hand in Polish, and was disinclined—in spite of the men's lively, tolerant attitude—to call any attention to himself, he picked up a newspaper that was nearest him, glancing at the front page which announced: HAYWOOD TRIAL IN JUNE.

From behind the curtain of his newspaper Pawel listened anxiously to the ongoing conversation, eager to learn what he could. But he soon realized that they were not talking about "freethinking" at all—they were talking about sports. Their hero of the hour it seemed, was John L. Sullivan, and the men were enthusiastically swapping opinions and comparing records: how many fights the great man had won compared to bouts other great fighters had won; and the men seemed to be as proud of the renowned fighter's prowess as if it had been their own.

But Pawel was jolted alert when, most unexpectedly, he heard the names of Prince Kropotkin and Bakunin. It was all he could do to keep from leaping to his feet and fleeing. . . . For a moment, he believed that he—and Bronís—had fallen into a trap. Perhaps this was the way they rounded up dissidents in America: by creating, as a decoy, an ostensibly free and open opinion forum, whereby all the self-incriminating speakers and visitors alike could be rounded up at once. He managed to stay put in his seat, however—merely swallowing his beer as calmly as he could. Just as at last he was about to permit himself to leave, he sat back in his seat again as he overheard what Bronís would be most anxious to have heard:

"That Slovak guy, you know? He's gonna talk tonight.

On Tom Paine. You want to come back? Not me, though—I'm not comin'. I'm too tired by then. But imagine this fellow—only a couple of years in this country and he's read every goddam book in the library. I guess he knows everything there is to know about those guys they hanged a few years back—"

"'*Few* years'! Time passes, Bob. Time passes. That was like a lifetime ago. Different world altogether. The working man—he's got some rights now. In your day, they couldn't have filled a tent with the IWWs. Now they're going to have a big meeting right here in Chicago."

"Whaddye mean 'my day'?" grumbled the other. I ain't that old. . . ."

They then began talking about the latest moving pictures. Had Bob seen the latest Chaplin picture? "Boy *that* was something!"

At this juncture, Pawel felt it safe to leave, but his heart was beating fast as he picked up his hat and made his way as nonchalantly as possible to the front of the saloon. He was thinking, with great relief, that he had made a safe exit from that ambiguous situation, when suddenly he felt a hand—gentle, but with a firmness reflecting a justified claim —touching his arm. Pawel halted, prepared to surrender himself.

"Hey, friend," said the man called Bob. "D'ye mind leavin' that paper? There's something in it about Haywood I meant to read." Then, at the look of surprise and dismay on Pawel's face, he added apologetically: "The club can't afford to buy enough papers for everybody."

With a slight tremor, Pawel handed over the paper he had somehow carried with him.

"Thanks, *amigo*," said Bob flipping open the paper. "Darrow's gonna defend him, y'know."

BUT WHILE IN THE CLUBROOM, Pawel had noticed a brief advertisement in a newspaper which, as a physician, had greatly interested him; so before boarding the train for Duluth the next day, he bought several newspapers—one in Polish—hiding them away in his valise until he could find a private moment to read them. As the train sped along Lake Michigan toward Wisconsin, he watched the disappearance of the great city with the gloom of an exile—longing, this time, not for his own country, but for the world he was now leaving behind him: one of theaters, art museums, concerts—a world, above all, of the companionship of educated men and, yes, women. But what woman, he asked himself—educated or not—would bind herself to a fugitive such as he was without even a proper identity of his own? He had heard that unmarried women in the West—indeed, even in the crowded cities of the East—were scarce as pearls. Yet, he thought, even if he were never to know the consolation of a woman's hand, he might have been able to find some peace of mind were he able to practice his own profession. But this Medea's cloak of disguise would eat away at his training until at last—as medical science advanced and he was left far behind—he would be nearly as ignorant again as when he had begun his studies as a boy of nineteen.

As if to confirm his dilemma, he opened a newspaper to exactly the sort of advertisement that had earlier seized his attention. It was an advertisement by a (Polish) physician who offered his prospective patients everything—freedom from heart palpitations, rheumatism, catarrh, bad skin (especially if caused by constipation), headache, fainting spells, and failing memory. . . . And the charlatan had the gall, thought Pawel, to address his immigrant countrymen in their native tongue, using his language as a quacking decoy. The appeal was highly personal, even hortatory, reminding his readers that he was the only physician they would find who, like them, spoke their language. The greedy rogue warned them, furthermore, not to delay seeking his help, lest they perish of some unknown disease: no one need hesitate to come to him, the impostor concluded with a flourish, because he offered *free* advice.

Pawel, upon reading this, sat back in his seat with disgust. Even in his own little village—hardly a spearhead of civilization—a single harsh rebuke from a *voyt* would have frightened such a mountebank right out of their village— the rascal perhaps feeling himself fortunate not to have had his coattails smeared with mud at the village terminus by an outraged populace. But, alas, what could he—Dr. Pawel Czarnocki—do? He could only hope that perhaps such thieves-of-life were to be found only in the crowded cities: he had read somewhere that the tenements of New York were comparable only to the teeming slums of Bombay; but perhaps in a place like Hibbings, with fewer people in the entire town than in one of those streets on the lower East Side, a doctor—if they had one at all, Pawel reflected—would be compelled to practice honest medicine, for fear there, as in Lunawicz, the village elders would rise to denounce him.

The advertisement had depressed him, but since the newspaper was, at least, in Polish, Pawel read each page greedily, savoring every word, including the plaintive letters to the editor: from parents complaining of their insubordinate children who refused to speak Polish (especially refusing to do so in the presence of American children); or from parents whose daughters stayed out late in the hallway "giggling with the boys," or parents whose children refused to turn over their week's earnings to their father, as they would have done in the Old Country. . . . And, finally, there was a letter to the editor from an irate citizen—but at this letter Pawel did not smile—demanding to know why a socialist agitator and notorious propagandist for the IWW like Elizabeth Gurley Flynn should be permitted to speak in Chicago's Brandt Hall. It was a pity, lamented the citizen, that Gurley Flynn was a U.S. citizen and therefore could not be deported; but at least such a dangerous woman ought to be put in prison along with all the others like her. . . .

Ah, politics, politics, sighed Pawel, feeling a wave of remorse over those whom he felt he had abandoned to the prisons of Russia. Then he closed his eyes wearily, hoping to sleep while the train sped toward Duluth.

UPON HIS ARRIVAL at Duluth, the fresh air, after the smell and grime of Chicago, comforted him, but he was surprised to find, that although it was mid-April, the piles of snow accumulated from previous storms had not yet completely melted. Also, in spite of the exhilarating freshness of the air, he felt visually assaulted by the great pyramids of coal piled up in the port like the mausoleums of some ancient city now silent and unpeopled. The dreariness of the endless coal was so depressing that he felt bereft even of his normal curiosity—he was simply anxious to get on with his journey and reach his destination at last. Thus it was with considerable gratitude that he managed to find a wagon driver with a pair of horses who was willing to take him that last sixty miles to Hibbings.

As they passed over mile after mile of roads rutted with

reddish mud from the red ore of the region, Pawel's heart sank with despair. To what outpost of desolation had Bronís brought him? In every town they passed through, he saw the blackened stumps of trees, the remains of great forests and lumber camps burnt out by forest fires, leaving only these charred skeletons as in some vast overturned grave. And surrounding this devastation in Dantean circles were the open-pit mines.

From his perch on the wagon above the pits Pawel could see what seemed to be miniature men on toy horses; and not far from these men were puffing little engines which, in spite of their small size, had created a veil of red haze. The whole scene struck Pawel as some image from the Maupassant story in which a malignant madness turns the world a burning red.

As they approached Hibbings, Pawel could hear the mine blastings clearly, and now—as the red curtain lifted— he could see steam shovels, like omnivorous prehistoric reptiles born again and evolved now into strange new animals with steel mouths and iron guts devouring the red earth.

His wagon driver now came to a stop at a row of tar-paper shacks, flung together with old planks and oil cans. Pigs grunted greedily as they rooted their snouts into the red mud. On the hillsides above, loomed great boulders, looking as if, at the next lightning bolt, they might come thundering down upon the tar-paper shacks.

Somewhat dazed by such an apparition, Pawel stepped down from the wagon and paid the driver. As he did so, the driver, looking toward the road ahead, pointed: Bronís could be seen in the distance, running toward them and waving excitedly.

"That must be your friend now, I guess. . . . Well, I

got you here, didn't I?" added the driver with a satisfied grin, and cracked his whip as he left Pawel in the muddy lane.

The old friends embraced, scanning each other's faces— for what? Pawel asked himself. For some sign perhaps that the fire of friendship was still warm—or that their old beliefs had not been utterly destroyed by the price they had been forced to pay for them. For moments they remained standing in the muddy lane, made silent by the flood of memories—of Lunawicz, of their years at grammar school, of Bronís' military service and his near-death in Russia, until at last Bronís said, with a new bitterness in his voice, "Ah, so you see how it is here, Pawel . . . the 'gold in the streets'?"

LATER, WHILE THEY sat over their dinner of potatoes and bacon, Bronís leaned his head in his hand as he said in an anxious tone, "You know that you might have to work in the pits?"

Pawel nodded somberly. But at the same time there spun through his head a clear recollection of an operating room: it, too, was a "pit"—an amphitheater—and he could hear again the teaching surgeon explaining to them how the physician must have hands that see—strong hands, yet sensitive as a bee's antennae. . . .

"Yes . . . I know—" he said at last, trying to look resigned.

"But the worst of it is," Bronís went on hesitantly, "that you can't even do *that* right now, because the guys are on strike. So, of course, you can't work . . . It would be dangerous for you. They get very angry. . . ."

Ah, no . . . , thought Pawel hotly. *No strikes. No, no,*

no, no. Scowling, he reminded Bronís of the repression his countrymen had already suffered from such notions. During the great strike of 1905, he had seen dozens of his countrymen bound and shackled and carried off to death or prison: no, he never wanted to see another strike as long as he lived. Such courage, such hope, such suffering—and then to have it all end with a few men—ignorant of the suffering that had gone before—enjoying a few *zlotys* more a day or perhaps slightly better working conditions, while the martyrs of the strike rotted in jail. He had come to regard with dread and suspicion the whole strategy of strikes: they now seemed to him to wreck the hopes of the very people they struggled for.

As Pawel mournfully reminded Bronís of these things, Bronís frowned, clearly not wanting to disagree with Pawel who had just arrived after a long and harsh journey; yet he could not help saying: "But conditions here are truly abominable. . . ." Sensing Pawel's rising resistance, however, to such talk, he interrupted himself quickly: "But you must be too tired from your long trip to talk of such things—you can't have slept on that train. I too had such a trip, only of course I was more fortunate than you, coming through Canada. Imagine! An almost empty country from one end to another, thousands of miles." Bronís shook his head at the recollection. "But I thought at first, there in Canada, it might be possible—in spite of my papers, you know—" he added, dropping his voice instinctively, although they were alone in his shack "—it might be possible . . . 640 acres for homesteading—if you're lucky enough to qualify . . . But when I began making inquiries, I drew such attention to myself from the authorities—I feared, you know . . . what can one do? Then one day, as I was standing in an employment office—Pawel, listen to this: this is what is happening to our countrymen—someone told me—I know now that he was standing there to recruit poor fools like us —that they needed workers here on the Iron Range. Though I'm not exactly an experienced worker"—here Bronís laughed bitterly as he referred to his military service where he had learned, he used to say, absolutely nothing except a few Russian curses—" of course I said yes: why not? Did I care whether I worked in a lumber camp or a mine? And they promised me three dollars a day. Well, Pawel, never mind. Needless to say, they didn't give me that much. But the worst thing about it—and this, how could I know?—they just wanted us ignorant foreigners to break the strike here. And they wanted people like me so bad—" here he laughed again, bitterly, "that, had I only known in time, I could have let you know, and you could have got your passageway paid for. You could have come free, *gratis*. . . ."

"I?" said Pawel in astonishment, setting down his glass of tea. "Even though I—?"

"Well, no, not exactly. Not with the 'even though'—*that* they would never excuse you here. But as Pawel Gabryszak, day laborer or farmer or whatever, they would have invited you to travel on a special ship—just for fools like Gabryszak —all the way to Canada. Then they would smuggle you across the border into the United States—also free, *gratis*, I presume—to work in the pits. They—the men they've smuggled over—they will be able to break this strike. But to think, Pawel, that it's our people, Slavs and Poles, who are being hired, and they're being insulted and threatened by the angry strikers, who, as you can imagine, hate them as if they were spies."

"But they don't know it, you say, when they come?" said Pawel defensively, somewhat taken aback by the epithet.

Bronís shook his head sadly. "What do they know about *anything* when they come? What's more—even their patriotism separates them from each other. The company tries to keep them apart—Poles from Russians, Finns from Croats. The stories they've told me. . . . Some kept in bull pens like cattle before being smuggled over the border. . . ."

"I think, Bronís . . . ," began Pawel with deliberate calm. "This is what I think. That you should stay out of this. This is not your fight! Your fight is for—" He knew he did not need to finish what he had begun to say.

"I know, I know," Bronís assured him quickly. "Yet it's hard—when you see your own people despised as strikebreakers not to be able to explain anything to them."

"There's nothing anymore to explain," said Pawel wearily. "It's . . . it's *history*, that's all . . . and inevitable. . . . As for me, I will do any work, any kind of work. But no more politics . . . not a word more."

Bronís smiled his disbelief. "OK, OK, as they say around here. You rest up now, then later I'll take you for a walk around our 'location.'" And he rose to prepare a cot for Pawel to sleep on. As he arranged the blankets for his friend, he began laughing as if at some reminiscence they shared. Pawel looked up inquiringly.

"Well—but at least the Russians are not much liked here either! Did you hear about Maxim Gorky and his woman? Last year they kicked both of them out of a hotel in New York—for not being married. . . ."

Pawel smiled for the first time in months and clapped his friend conspiratorially on the back as he eased himself into bed.

184

AFTER ABOUT A WEEK of walking around the town, Pawel felt he had been there for months: he had talked to so many foreign workers that he felt it only a matter of time before there would be a half-dozen new churches in the town. One thing troubled him, however: because so many of the strikebreakers were, like himself, in the country illegally, they asked no questions; on the other hand they did not speak to him openly and trustingly, as they had spoken to Bronís of their hegira across the border, because they had been warned—Bronís had told him—that informers sometimes infiltrated their numbers, and if they were to be discovered, they would be summarily deported to the Old Country. And although they quietly accepted Pawel's presence there, there remained between them and himself an air of reserve, a suspicion—traceable perhaps to Pawel's manner of speaking, in which language flowered here and there into an eloquence at which his countrymen would merely stare at him blankly.

Bronís took him everywhere, introducing him as a cousin. It was only natural, everyone had a cousin or brother: what they needed, their countrymen would say with a laugh, were not more cousins, but wives. Did Pawel perhaps have a sister in the Old Country?

To this Pawel would only smile collusively, retorting that he, too, needed a wife to warm his bed. But though Pawel smiled, it was only too true: he too needed a wife; he suffered much from loneliness; he wished someone would introduce him to a sister from the Old Country. As Bronís showed him around the mining camp, he could not help noticing that the few unmarried women living there seemed delighted with his presence, greeting him as warmly as the proprieties permitted. But Pawel dared not approach any one of them in a personal, social way, for fear that from a moment's trusting confidence his secret might soon sound through the town like an alarm bell.

Nowhere was Pawel more warmly received than at the house of Janek Moraski, whose daughter Domicella, he was told, was now slowly recovering from a long winter's bout with influenza. But to Pawel's practiced eye, the girl seemed to him tubercular: she had complained to her father of feverish sweats at night; her cheeks remained flushed with a spurious radiance Pawel knew too well, and even as he and Bronís stood at the door, they could hear the girl's racking, intermittent cough. Before they left him, Moraski asked Bronís if he would stop off at the drugstore for some cough medicine for his daughter. Pawel averted his eyes as he saw the worried miner lay the money for the medicine in Bronís' hand; and when they had walked to the drugstore, Pawel—still brooding over the girl—refused to accompany Bronís to the rear of the drugstore where, he was certain, the pharmacist would pour more, "cough syrup" into a little glass bottle for Domicella's illness. Instead, he stood impatiently enough at the entrance, where a young clerk was managing the cash register and filling the shelves nearby with familiar items. Pawel—with a profound bitterness not unmixed with longing—gazed around him: the most rudimentary tools of his trade—bandages, scissors, iodine—were here displayed like holy relics, side by side with the usual poultices and patent medicines that claimed to cure everything from morning sickness to apoplexy. Without amusement (nor even disdain: he felt himself involved in a tragedy, not a Molièresque farce), he picked up a bottle of ROMKO, which the clerk had prominently displayed in the front aisle. The placard read: FOR EVERY

MOTHER, and beneath this sign was a photograph of two infants—one in apparent misery while the mother walked the floor in the middle of the night, the other of an infant as blissful as a Christmas angel. ROMKO—he read—was a "certain medicine for crying and sleeplessness," and, at a price of only thirty-five cents for a bottle of ROMKO, manufactured by the Baby Safety Company, no mother should allow her baby to suffer for hours. . . .

Pawel turned away in disgust, but while he stood there, he saw one of Bronís' neighbors actually pay thirty-five cents for the so-called medicine: it was all he could do not to put out a restraining hand.

"And did you get the cough medicine for Domicella?" demanded Pawel with bitter irony when Bronís returned.

Shamefacedly, Bronís held up the bottle of red syrup.

While they were waiting for the clerk to wrap up a few small items Bronís had purchased, an elderly man strolled up behind them. Whether it was because of his clothes or the aura of calm self-possession, there was something familiar about him: he reminded Pawel of the well-dressed professional men whom he had met while a medical student. That strangers should seem familiar had now become habitual to Pawel: several times already he had thought he recognized people he had once known. It was a sort of hallucination, perhaps, born of his deep longing to meet someone from home who might give him news of his lost world. The feeling was usually evoked by some prosaic item he knew well—a woman in a shawl, a weatherworn face, men in their boots. And whenever this familiarity struck him, he would closely watch the person's face for some sign of recognition, in the vague hope that the person was, like himself, only a political refugee in disguise, someone who was trying perhaps to send him a message from oblivion—an assurance that Maks or Franciszek or Tomasz was still alive.

But whatever this elderly man may once have been, Pawel thought, he was clearly not at the present time a peasant: he was dressed from head to toe like a wealthy American. Pawel only wished the man would speak, for though he might look like an American-born, if he were to speak, Pawel felt certain he would recognize his accent: a man could change his clothes, but he could not so readily change his language, and if the elderly man were to say something to the clerk, Pawel might, at least, recognize the sounds of his own country.

But the stranger did not or would not speak: he was totally absorbed in the selection of several cigars from a box on the counter; and when he had made his choice, he handed them silently to the clerk. As the three men then headed for the street, Bronís politely held open the door for the older man, and the stranger nodded his thanks; then he stood outside the drugstore lighting his cigar.

As they headed back to Janek's house with the medicine, Pawel asked: "That man you opened the door for—do you know him?"

Bronís shrugged his ignorance, but added with a shrewd look: "Probably out looking for IWWs among the strikers. They hate them, of course. . . . I'm told they've got people with guns, just to scare them away. I guess they're nervous, with that Haywood trial about to start soon, only a few hundred miles from here."

Pawel did not ask who "they" were—he was determined to avoid politics—but he reflected with a smile of admiration at his friend on how quickly Bronís was becoming an

American: for the distance, he estimated roughly, from Hibbings to Boise, would have taken him from Lunawicz to Germany. . . .

Pawel was about to make some joke about Bronís rapid Americanization when Bronís abruptly excused himself— he had to get back to the grain and feed store he was temporarily working in: would Pawel mind taking Domicella's medicine to Moraski's house? He had promised Janek to bring it as soon as possible.

"Yes, of course," said Pawel angrily, gripping the bottle as if he were about to smash it at their feet, "I'll take Domicella her . . . *medicine!*"

IT WAS THE first time he had ever visited Janek without Bronís, and he felt somewhat ill-at-ease. His concern for Domicella might well be misinterpreted. It had been only too sadly clear to him, that were he visiting Moraski as a possible suitor, he would have been warmly welcomed by the family.

He found Janek at home as he had expected (besides being one of the strikers, he rarely left Domicella alone). As Pawel set the bottle of syrup beside Domicella's bed, Janek offered him a drink. When Pawel refused—perhaps too politely—Janet gave him an odd look, but made no comment except to apologize for the muddy roads Pawel had had to walk through to reach their house. "But it will be summer soon, and you will see—everything will dry up— it will be better, yes?"

While Janek bustled around the shack looking for a spoon—he was sorry, he said that his wife was not here to greet Pawel, but she had gone looking for some fresh eggs to make a spring tonic for Domicella—Pawel sat at Domicella's bedside. He nodded gravely at Janek's words. His eyes were on the girl: she seemed even more listless than she had been the week before, and, in spite of her obvious efforts to control her coughing, she would turn away now and then from Pawel, racked by a harsh and ruthless seizure. He wanted to speak to Janek about his daughter, but felt he could say nothing in her presence; so he sat, silent and humbled, reflecting on her condition. As he looked around the shack he was filled with a helpless rage: there was a small stove in the room which clearly had not been lit, though the cold air drove like nails from under the door. Although some attempt had once been made at elegance and modesty—thick lace curtains covered the cracked windows, and on the table beside Domicella's bed there was a red geranium in a coffee tin—from where he sat, Pawel could see the outdoor privies and the muddy lanes. His imagination faltered as he tried to imagine the Moraskis' attempt to care for their sick child all winter long in a tarpaper shack without the most primitive accommodations. In despairing silence, he sat holding Domicella's hand, forgetful even that he had no right to do so, being neither her betrothed nor her physician.

As if sensing the reason for Pawel's silence, Janek remarked suddenly, as if they had been carrying on their conversation: "And Pecia will get Domicella some milk, too."

Pawel watched helplessly as Janek adjusted Domicella's pillow and helped her to sit up—as gently as any nurse in Berlin, thought Pawel—and then poured out some of the thick red syrup into a tablespoon. Domicella swallowed the liquid obediently, almost eagerly—as if she believed that indeed this medicine would at last make her well. In her haste, a red droplet spilled down her shirtwaist, and as it rolled toward her chest, like some sweet red gumball filled with opium, Pawel felt such an overwhelming premonition of Domicella's syrup-coated death that he exclaimed with sudden passion: "Janek, I *must* talk to you. I must talk to you privately—." His voice broke and he could say nothing more in the presence of the girl.

Janek looked around the shack in wonder—the very concept of privacy, Pawel saw, was alien to him. But, patting his daughter's arm reassuringly, he rose in response to Pawel's clear need to speak to him alone, and, taking down his jacket from where it hung on a nail, he beckoned Pawel outside.

As they walked through the muddy lanes strewn with bits of garbage or with ashes from the iron stoves, Pawel stopped suddenly and, facing Janek, began—stammering with passion—to tell him what he must do if he wanted to save his daughter from almost certain death. At first, Janek listened to him with an expression of tolerant sorrow, as if listening to a madman or perhaps a desperate suitor for Domicella's hand; then, as Pawel, nearly weeping with desperation, spoke rapidly of the need for a sanitarium, for a dry climate, for a place where Domicella would be regularly and properly cared for, a place where she might have examinations and X-rays and sputum counts and even, perhaps, if it were necessary, pneumothorax surgery to collapse her lung—Janek began to understand that Pawel knew far more of medicine than the home remedies of a farmer, and he began abruptly to sob aloud. Then, to Pawel's astonishment, Janek kneeled in the mud and, crossing himself reverently, murmured in a deeply prayerful tone: "Ah, thanks be to God. He has sent us a doctor—one of our own. Our Domicella will get well. . . ."

B<small>OTH</small> M<small>ORASKI AND</small> P<small>AWEL</small> tried to keep it a secret. But when, upon heeding some of Pawel's more immediate and practicable advice (Pawel's urgent suggestion that Domicella be moved to a sanitarium, preferably in a warm climate, was, Moraski had mourned, all very well, but who was to pay for it?) of fresh milk every day, more fresh air and sunshine, much bedrest, and all the nourishment Domicella's listless appetite would accept, Domicella seemed to become stronger, the entire town soon learned somehow that there was a new immigrant from the Old Country who knew certain up-to-date medical secrets. Whether he was a true physician was immaterial to them: he spoke their language, and his advice, therefore, was more satisfying to their souls, if nothing else, than any medicine they had received elsewhere. Before he realized it, dozens of people from the town were stopping by Bronís' shack, ostensibly only to introduce themselves to Bronís' cousin from their homeland, but—like the returning veterans and prisoners of Lunawicz—remaining to ease their burdens by talking, and concluding their visit, finally, by showing Pawel an infection that had taken root, a bruise or lump that had not gone away. When, eventually, Pawel was called upon to set a broken leg, and did so so expertly that the miner was soon able to hobble along the wooden boardwalk Pawel had built outside his shack, Pawel's reputation was fixed forever in the minds of the miners and their wives.

The people of the town firmly believed they now had their own doctor, and tried to pay him—the women by stopping by to bring him a cabbage or by taking his clothes to wash, the men by bringing him coal for his stove, or by fixing his leaking roof. And when Bronís warned Pawel repeatedly that he *must* stop, that this could not go on, Pawel agreed at once that Bronís was right. But, he added, waving his arms helplessly, when his own countrymen came to him, begging him to listen to their troubles, how could he turn them away? Once, during one of these arguments, in order to remind Pawel of the fury of their enemy, Bronís had rolled back his shirt sleeves and silently shown Pawel his scars from the manacles of Russia. And, as always, Pawel had agreed that, yes, Bronís was right, he must stop. . . .

So for Pawel, it was a heartfelt blessing that on the morning that they came to seize him, Bronís was away. The men who came were not rude or brutal: with their badges, and their guns resting in their holsters, they had no reason to raise their voices. In the grey morning light, Pawel could barely see their faces, but he heard very distinctly, as if it had been the crack of a stone-breaking hammer, the voice of a man saying in his native tongue, "That's the one."

As they drove away in the carriage, Pawel sat between a tall man wearing a red plaid jacket and an elderly man who somehow reminded him of other men he had known but whose names he could not recall, men with faces of universal anonymity, so that one met them again and again— on a train, on board ship, in a drugstore or restaurant. But this elderly stranger was not silent like the others but rather was reciting softly now, with remarkable correctness, the litany of Dr. Pawel Czarnocki's crimes: a forged passport, a convicted anarchist in his own country, practicing medicine under an assumed name. . . .

As he listened to the murmured accusations, Pawel

closed his eyes, leaning back in the carriage. His attention was drawn at that moment, not to the sound of the elderly man's voice but to the sound of the horses' hooves: and there flashed across his memory, as in a historic diorama, an image of the palace of Peter the Great; and in front of the palace were the dissidents whom the Czar had ordered to be buried alive up to their necks and then to be executed by the furious trampling of horses over their miserable heads. . . .

Ah Maks, his heart cried out silently to his old friend, *I'm coming to you.* But he thought long afterwards that he must have spoken aloud, evoking by the very force of his love Maks' physical presence. For as the horses galloped ever onward, he could see with luminous clarity Maks and himself shackled together on the floor of their prison— alert and ready and listening—to fiery explosions, the crack of gunshot, and the thundering roar of millions of voices as the walls of their prison turned to smoke.

A Note about the Author

Natalie L. M. Petesch has published nine previous books of fiction including five novels and four short story collections. She lives in Pittsburgh with her husband, Donald Petesch, who teaches American literature at the University of Pittsburgh.